A THOUSAND DREADFUL CURSES

A THOUSAND DREADFUL CURSES

Editing by Silvia Curry
Cover and Interior Design by We Got You Covered Book Design
www.wegotyoucoveredbookdesign.com

A THOUSAND DREADFUL CURSES

JACOB DEVLIN

"Fill the world with music, love and pride."
LIN-MANUEL MIRANDA

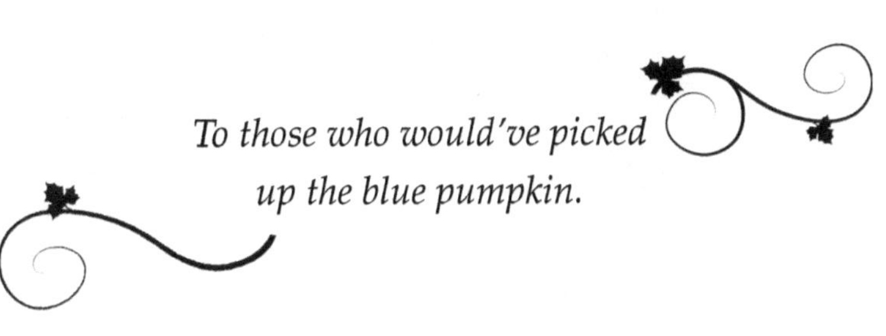

To those who would've picked up the blue pumpkin.

SATURDAY, OCTOBER 25

THE CURSE OF LABYRINTHS

ONE

JACK

Tonight is my first time being cursed. And so far, the experience isn't meeting my expectations.

In defiance of everything I ever expected, a silver moon gleams in a cloudless sky and a pleasant breeze tickles my arms. Crops surround me endlessly, stalks of corn swaying in the wind. I listen to the husks rustling and imagine them whispering gossip to each other.

Did you hear about Prince Jack? Cursed by the Winter Queen herself and banished from the Kingdom of Veron! On his own wedding day!

You don't say! What happened to him? Is he trapped in an ice palace? Has his heart been frozen? Does he vomit snow when he becomes ill?

No, he's wandering a labyrinth made of corn.

When I awoke here, my boots had lost some of their shine and my clothes were covered in dust, but I assumed that would be the least of my problems. I blinked the dreary haze from my vision, bolted to my feet, and put my hand to my dagger.

I was supposed to wake up in a vinecrawler's belly or at least have to fight one when I woke up. Samuel, my mentor, has been training me all my life for the worst case scenarios. He taught me all sorts of dagger techniques in case I ever confronted a vinecrawler in a foul mood.

For three hours, I've traversed the labyrinth ready for combat. Everyone knows that any properly cursed maze must contain a monster of some sort. In this one, not even so much as a rat stirs, and there's food all around me.

The Winter Queen is the worst at designing curses.

Samuel and I discussed many scenarios— loss of all my senses, combat against an army of creatures, adverse weather from the gods, and anything else we could brainstorm together. A thousand possible curses. It's not like Samuel has actually lived through one—he's just a spectacular fighter with a brilliant mind.

Maybe he should've trained me for severe boredom. As I wander the labyrinth, I weave a story in my mind. When I go home, I'll tell everyone I faced a giant vinecrawler . . . with all my senses removed . . . in a snowstorm.

And then I'll roast the Winter Queen on an open flame until she melts.

Of course, there are a few other problems I'll have to deal with. Repairing my social reputation and dealing with the whole *runaway groom* thing. I'll have to apologize to Aurora and my family and generally recover from a world of guilt. But I guess it's like what Samuel says about chess—take the queen move by move.

Step one: Clear the labyrinth.

The Winter Queen wasn't very specific. Is this how I free myself? Seven days or less to solve the maze, and then I return home? Because that seems too simple. Sure, by day three, I'll go mad with frustration. My feet may bleed. My legs may cry out for me to stop walking. But there are darker curses to bear.

There's the fable about the boy who lived as a wooden puppet until he learned to stop lying.

There are the children who ate the house of sweets, then nearly became a witch's dinner.

There's the princess who accepted a suspicious fruit from a stranger and fell asleep for a very long time. Technically, I suppose she was dead, but it was all sorted out in the end.

I don't mean to shame the heroes of the fables. However, their curses were grand and possibly beneficial. Stars and gods know I could catch up on about five years of sleep. I would also enjoy an apple or some type of sugary snack.

But no, I'm cursed to be Prince Jack of the Corn Labyrinth. The bards will record my story and bind it into books, and all the kids will say, "Please, Mother, can we skip this one? Read the one about the wooden puppet instead."

As I wander, I carve tiny notches into the corn stalks, so I'll recognize them if I'm walking in circles. I got the idea when I passed the same scarecrow twice, the silver moon illuminating its hollow eye sockets. For hours, this scarecrow has been my only company in this forsaken field.

"Hey!" someone calls, nearly prying my spirit from my body.

I'm not alone after all, and I'm not sure if this is a good thing.

I turn around and find a family of four, all dressed in peculiar garb. Their faces have been painted with mouse-like whiskers and dark, shiny noses. They wear black clothes and wide, round circles on their heads. Mouse ears, I suppose? One of them wears a large polka-dotted bow, and she stares daggers at me with her hands on her hips.

"You shouldn't destroy the corn like that," she says. "This is a farm."

I sheath my dagger and scrub my hand over my forehead, hardly daring to believe my eyes. Cautiously, I take a step toward the family.

"Hello there," I say. "Have you been cursed as well? Has the Winter Queen sent you here?"

The two eldest mouse people exchange funny glances, and the woman breaks into a grin. "Ah, you must be one of the actors. I'm sorry to lecture you. I adore your costume, by the way. Are you Prince Charming?"

"Charming?" I step back. "No, ma'am, I'm Prince Jack! Why are you here?"

The two children giggle. "We're trying to solve the corn maze, silly!"

"So you are cursed," I say. "The Winter Queen must pay for what she's doing to our people. Perhaps we can help each other."

"Boy, he's really in character," Mother Mouse says. "Too cute. Happy Halloween, hon. I hope you find your princess!"

Mother Mouse guides her family deeper into the maze, leaving me with nothing but questions.

What in the stars is Hollow Wene? And what princess?

Aurora must be here. Would the Winter Queen really curse her own daughter?

"Wait!" I rush after the family.

My heart leaps from my chest when a rotting monstrosity flies out of the corn stalks and chases the family. "*Rawr!*"

I've never seen anything like it. The fear roots me to the ground. The monstrosity is about my height and built like the average man, but its face is a mess of something like green leather, wrinkled and painted in scars. White clumps of hair spring from its scalp in odd patches. It wears a tattered shirt, tight blue trousers, and white leather footwear with a peculiar black symbol on them.

"I'm gonna get you!" the monstrosity cries in a surprisingly human voice. It raises its hands high over its head and follows the family into the corn.

I never should've let my guard down. There *are* horrors in this maze—just not the kind I'd expected. No vinecrawlers or dragons, but Samuel never prepared me for rotting green monsters. However, this is what's expected of a prince—selflessly saving others in need, dashing to the rescue, and protecting the kingdom.

My hand goes to my dagger.

"I'll save you!" I sprint after the monstrosity. "Halt, green horror! I command you in the name of the king!" *Not that I expect the name of King Harold to mean anything here.*

The family squeals, giggles, and turns a corner. To my surprise, the monstrosity slows down, turns away, and lowers its hands to its knees. It crouches low and takes deep, long breaths.

And without a word, the monstrosity reaches up and proceeds to remove its face.

A thick sheet of green comes off with no tearing, no gore, no resistance. Instead of a skull, the monstrosity reveals a second layer of skin, fair with patches of green around the eyes. Dark wavy hair plastered to its face in sweat. The monstrosity looks decidedly human now—not so different from myself.

I approach him slowly, my hand hovering over my weapon. I'm thinking of all the maneuvers I can do to incapacitate him when he looks up and runs his fingers through his hair. "Gotta catch my breath, bro." He stares into the hollow green face he holds in his hands. "Don't mind me. It's been a long night of scaring."

"Your face…" I manage to say, looking between his old face and his new one. "What kind of creature are you?"

The guy lets out something like a tired laugh and shakes his head. "Heh. I'm a zombie. Rawr!" He holds up his old face and wiggles two fingers through the parted lips. It's rather grotesque. "And you? Let me guess … Prince Charming?"

There's that name again. Who is this *Charming* fellow?

"I'm Prince Jack," I say. "Why did you attack that kind family? Are you cursed, too?"

The man laughs again. "Heh, you're funny. I'm working on a Saturday night. Of course I'm cursed. I could be at home playing the new *Galaxy's Oceans*." He eyes my dagger and his jaw drops. "Hey, how'd you sneak that in here? No weapons allowed, real or fake. I gotta confiscate your knife. You can have it back at the exit."

I clench my fists at the audacity. "You're taking my *dagger*? You are an ally of the Winter Queen. Where is she?"

The monstrosity rolls his eyes and holds out his hand.

This knife is special, carefully built to withstand the strongest of curses. I only give it over because I could stand a modest challenge. If there's no vinecrawler or dragon, then there must be *some* glory in this curse.

"Sure, man. I'm an ally of the Winter Queen, if that's what you call Elaine. I'm just gonna take this weapon back to her at Dreamland Castle." He scoffs and turns his back to me. "I don't get paid nearly enough for this."

He lies. He mocks me. Nev, the Winter Queen, would never pay her allies.

I lose the monstrosity a few minutes later, distracted by new families and groups who arrive in short intervals. People dress so strangely—like large pink rabbits, pirates, ghosts, and even fried eggs—yet they never seem to play the role they dress for. The ghosts don't phase through corn stalks. The pirates don't try to rob me. Instead, they all wish me a 'Happy Hollow Wene.'

And one by one, they chip away at my patience when they ask if I'm Prince Charming.

This is my curse. I'm surrounded by strange people who think I'm someone else entirely.

"I'm Jack Zuka," I declare to no one in particular. "Prince Jack of the Kingdom of Veron! Not *Charming*. And I will break this curse once and for all."

As the night wears on, I breathe a little heavier and my face grows warmer than normal. I'm bored. I'm annoyed. I'm confused.

I'm worried. If I'm not home to defend Veron, who besides Samuel is protecting my family?

Make no mistake, my mother is fierce. If the Winter Queen has her sights on my family, my mother will go down swinging, and not before making Nev's life miserable. I used to say the same about my father, but everyone knows the king is not at full strength. His health wanes by the day, and Veron scrambles to make preparations for his successor—me.

But did I even ask to be the future king?

Strangely, I'm almost relieved to be here. In this place, where nobody knows who I am, how high can their expectations be? Do they care who I marry, what kind of throne I sit on, or how polished my boots are? I'm almost gratified to hear people get my name wrong.

Almost.

Time stretches and crawls on for the rest of the night. The moon drifts closer to the horizon, the stars swirl above me, and I don't see another living soul. And no matter how many Xs I make in the corn stalks, how many turns I make, or how far I walk, I keep passing the same stupid scarecrow, over and over again.

Overcome with boredom and frustration, I finally plant myself on the ground. I lie there and think of the future. Tiny pebbles dig into my bones and make the ground terribly uncomfortable, but my muscles find a smidge of wonder and relief.

I have seven days. Only seven.

Think, Jack, think.

I stare up at the skies, which slowly turn pink with the promise of coming sunlight. I want out of this labyrinth, but deep down, I don't know if I want home, either. I want companionship, but I don't know if I want Aurora. I want people to stop calling me Prince Charming, but I don't want my responsibilities as Prince Jack.

I want something different.

And I don't know how to articulate it except to whisper one word.

"Help," I breathe to the rising sun.

Instead, pain comes.

I remember feeling this sensation when the Winter Queen uttered her curse—a tingle shooting down my spine and into my palms and feet. A total stiffness that roots me to the Earth. I sort of blacked out the first time it happened, but my newfound adrenaline gives my muscles just enough life to tilt my head off the ground. I'm puzzled by what I see.

I'm turning blue. Frosted, ghostly winter blue.

My arms fold into my body like accordions and my legs shrink into my torso. The world around me expands, every corn stalk suddenly reaching for the stars. I simply can't move any more. I can't talk. I can't breathe. I can't wiggle my toes.

My senses leave me one by one. My vision fades to black. My ears feel like they've been plugged with wet cotton. My nose sinks into my face and my lips melt shut, binding my tongue to the roof of my mouth. My mind pools into goo.

What am I becoming?

I don't know, but I wonder if maybe the Winter Queen has had the last laugh after all.

SUNDAY, OCTOBER 26

THE CURSE OF WOUNDS AND WINTERS

TWO

ISAAC

Freshman year is weird. Relationships are weird. Freshman year relationships are weirdness squared, but the most complicated part comes after they end.

This is what I discover in the backseat of my best friend Armand's car. I'm squished against the window with my ex and his new girlfriend, Sun. Seth sits in the middle, and his elbow's been bumping against mine for the past half hour while he engages in tickle wars with my *other* best friend. I probably should've called shotgun to avoid all this.

I rest my head against the window. We said this wouldn't be weird, and what makes me mad is that for Seth, the ride probably isn't weird at all. He probably feels so smug and satisfied squished between us, so warm and cozy snuggled between his old flame and his new one. He has the best of both worlds while my world still feels broken.

Armand glances at me in the rearview mirror, and I can read his expression. '*You doing all right back there?*'

I flash him a weak smile and he accelerates the car ever-so-slightly. "Isaac, you're riding shotgun on the way home."

What a bro.

Miranda turns down the music. "You said what now?"

"Pilot's choice," Armand says. "It's gonna be his turn."

"He has to call it," Miranda says. "Shotgun rules. There's no *pilot's choice*."

"His legs are longer and he has better taste in music," Armand counters.

Miranda taps her chest. "You're gonna tell the only musician in the group that she doesn't have the best taste in music? What is this madness?"

"Isaac does have better taste," Sun says.

"Wow, you all are the worst." Miranda turns

around and raises a brow at Seth. "Don't you side with them. I will end you."

Seth blinks a few times, fidgeting with his seatbelt. "No comment. Armand, please don't make me sit next to Miranda on the way home. She's scary." He turns to me. "Isaac, don't leave me."

Something about that phrase hurts, but I bury the pain and smirk at Miranda. "We'll see who calls it after we get our pumpkins."

We'd been planning to hit Farmer Elaine's Pumpkin Patch for a few weeks now—since *before* the breakup. The thing is, I almost didn't come with the group today on account of the weirdness, but FOMO got the best of me. If I didn't come, it'd be a slippery slope. I'd decline one hangout, and then another, and another, and Seth would forget me completely and our circle of five would close up and become a circle of four. And that's not a circle at all; it's a square, and I would just be a little dot on the outside. So here I am, stewing in the awkwardness.

"So what's the first thing we wanna do when we get there?" Armand asks.

"Hayride!" Miranda says. "Always hayride."

She cranks the music back up and waves her arms in the air like a hayride is on the same level of fun as the beach party the song is referring to.

"We have to get the popcorn, too," Sun says. "They always have such fun flavors! Lemon poppyseed, chili, horchata . . . .. I heard they're piloting pumpkin spice this year and it's supposed to be really good."

"Do we really need more pumpkin spice-flavored things?" Seth asks. "Hey, Sun, I'll share some with you."

I hate everything.

"No. Get your own," Sun says.

Everything is awesome.

"Fine. Isaac will share with me." Seth makes a sad puppy dog face at me. "Won't you, pwease?"

I can't look at that expression, not when it used to mean so many other things to me that we'll never share again. Secrets. Ice cream. Really good hugs. I shake my head. "Nope. I'll share with Sun," I say.

Sun reaches over Seth to high five me, then blows him a raspberry.

In the rearview mirror, Armand flashes me

a knowing smile.

I spring out of the car when we arrive, thankful for the new leg room and crisp air.

A typical Belhaven summer is humid, and it's like I can feel the air holding its breath. Then October comes around and lets out this big sigh, turning everything red, orange, and gold—and I mean everything. Around September, I swear it's like a costume shop explodes and spills its guts everywhere. The town pops with rubber bats in trees, tiny skulls adorning spiked fences, and pumpkins all over the streets.

And Farmer Elaine is not immuneto Halloween Fever. The first stop is her barn, where an inflatable witch protrudes from the wall. She sits on a broomstick with her arms spread out as if she's crashed into the barn, her pointy hat all askew and her ruby-slippered legs dangle over our heads. When we're close enough to walk beneath her, a recording plays, "Oh, drat! Life can be such a witch!"

Sun giggles, pulls out her phone, and points it at the witch. "Oh my goodness, that's so cute!"

Inside the barn, a crew of costumed

workers sit at a row of tables as the *Monster Mash* plays on the radio. A strobe light flickers, though the effect is masked by too much sunlight. At the first table, a plump woman in flowy silk dances a little jig, her bangles ringing as she waves her arms. Next to her cash box, a crystal ball swirls with glittering mist. As soon as she sees me, she freezes and points to me. "Saw you comin' in my crystal ball, honey! Your whole life's about to change today."

I play along. "Sweet! Am I about to become a millionaire?"

"Even better." The woman waves her hands over the ball. "You're about to enjoy a day on my farm! What could possibly be more magical? You don't need to be a millionaire to feel rich, you know."

This must be Farmer Elaine. I humor her and throw up a fist. "Yay."

Farmer Elaine ushers the rest of the group over. "Welcome, my loves. It's gonna be the *best* day."

Miranda squints at the crystal ball. "What did you see in our futures, miss?"

Farmer Elaine opens her cash box and

holds out her palm. "Y'all are about to give me twenty-five dollars."

Miranda leaps away from the table. "Each?"

Armand gestures to a sign on the wall.

ADMISSION = $5.00. INCLUDES CORN MAZE AND HAYRIDES!

"Phew!" Miranda brushes an arm across her forehead.

We hand over our cash while a skull-faced cowboy tears some paper wristbands for us.

A worker in a Bo Peep costume points her crook in Elaine's direction. "Oh, she's good. Madame, can you tell us if it's going to rain tomorrow? I'm thinking of washing my car after we close."

"I'd hold off," Elaine says, suddenly serious. "The news say it's gonna storm somethin' fierce on Friday."

"Ooh, that's Halloween," the cowboy says.

"And a full moon. You heard it here first, hon." When our wristbands are secure, Elaine wiggles her fingers at us, her bracelets jangling. "Enjoy, okay?"

And so we exit through the doors opposite

where we came in, and we enter the world of Elaine's farm. My nose immediately detects food—a delicious mingling of funnel cakes and apple pie. Various booths advertise fried pickles, nachos, cider, and popcorn.

Kids whiz around in costumes, faces sticky with a mixture of cotton candy and face paint. A pair of horses pull a train into the distant field, the passengers nestled on bricks of hay. Local vendors advertise everything from autumn-themed cookbooks to leather boots, purses, and face masks. Armand wastes no time breaking away from us to check out the lady with the dragon merch—puppets, coloring books, and pewter figurines.

"Let's take a picture!" Miranda breaks out her phone again. "Armand, get back here."

We form a huddle outside the barn and appoint Armand to be the selfie-taker because his arms are the longest.

We're a cute little group, I admit. Sun and I have known each other since sixth grade when her family moved to Belhaven from Los Angeles. I was assigned her "lunch buddy," which almost never works out when it's forced, but we quickly hit it off over our mutual love of The Vegas Thunderlings, an indie rock band who knows my soul. See, it's not just the deep lyrics about love and life— it's also the lead singer, Chris D'Agosto, who happens to be all over Sun's binder as a cluster of fading stickers. He also happens to be all over my bedroom walls as a cluster of pull-out magazine posters, but here's the thing . . . Sun didn't know that at first, and my parents . . . well, they were gracious enough to play along when I said, "I just really admire his songwriting."

Cue junior high, when nothing makes sense and we're all our most complicated, awkward selves.

Basically, Sun and I went to Skate Town together one night, and during a particularly schmaltzy slow song, she confessed deeper feelings for me. And seventh grade Isaac was funneling *all* his energy into pretending he liked sports and rationalizing those Chris D'Agosto posters on the wall. I told myself Chris was *just* an admirable drummer and not some demigod with the face of a Disney prince, the voice of Jesus, and the muscles of Thor. And therefore, it made all the sense in the world to date Sun.

Truth: I love Sun. I'd do anything for her. She's beautiful inside and out.

Lies I tried to stuff into the truth: Sun is my one and only. She sets my heart on fire. I'm *in* love with her.

The lines get so sticky when best friends date, and Sun was the first person I ever dated. The truths were powerful enough that I felt right dating her. Then the lies took all my headspace trying to become truths, and a week later, I couldn't sleep. I bombed an algebra test. My mom wanted to know why I was so moody.

Sun and I broke up eight days into our short relationship because I kissed her, and I just *knew*. I knew I'd never feel the spark that Sun felt, and if I couldn't feel it for her, I'd never feel it for any girl. So I worked up the courage to come out, which understandably hurt Sun's feelings. We stopped talking for three months. I came out to my parents, who were incredibly chill about it and never brought up the D'Agosto posters. A giant weight fell off my shoulders. The loneliness was still heavy, but I think it had been there all along. Not because Sun wasn't great company, but because I was keeping a part of myself from her and everyone else my life. It was like nobody knew me in the first place. But finally, I knew myself, and so did others.

Coincidentally, as Sun's original "lunch buddy," I found myself eating alone for a while. But that's how I found Armand. One day we just ended up at opposite ends of the same table, each alone in our own worlds. He used to have this kind of gothic thing going on—guyliner, a spiky belt, and black everything—and I guess it freaked people out. I didn't care. He was so content in his bubble of headphones, a sketchbook, and a little Ziplock full of sour gummy worms. I wanted a gummy worm and offered to trade for an Oreo, and then I realized he was drawing one of my favorite video game characters and I wanted to see more of his sketchbook. It turned out he was listening to K-Pop, which caught me by surprise because I had assumed he'd be listening to death metal or something. By the time the bell rang, we were bros, and the rest is history.

As the Isaac and Armand era was developing

over video games, snacks, and the casual exchange of musical tastes, Sun was forming a beautiful friendship with Miranda Cortez. I don't know all the details, except that when Sun and I made up over spring break, our separate duos became a team of four, and I loved it. Sun and I picked up without missing a beat. She and Armand had to warm up to each other a bit—I'm not sure if it was best-friend-jealousy or the goth thing, but it all worked out. As for Miranda, I appreciated the pep she added to our group. She always wanted to document our lunches with pictures, show off her bass guitar skills, and introduce new board games to us on the weekends.

Eighth grade—Armand went to high school, and while we were bummed we had to spend a year without him in school, we all still hung out on weekends. His freshman year washed out his goth phase, and he made a sophomore friend who could drive us around until Armand was of age. That driver was Seth, and he was *everything*.

I stare at the photo of all of us. It's one I want to frame. Our little group. Our found family.

The group makes some potty breaks, leaving Sun outside with me. She wastes no time pulling me to the side, and I already know what she's about to do.

Sun puts her hands on her hips. "You're not okay, are you?"

I play dumb because this is an awkward time to get into it. "What do you mean?"

Sun pulls up our group photo and points to me. "How long have we known each other? I know when you're not okay, and this picture says it all."

Seeing myself from the outside, Sun has a point.

For starters, I'm wearing a baseball cap, and that's a weird thing. If there's one thing about my looks that I'm proud of, it's my shiny dark hair. On a normal day, I spend some time on it. Lately, I just towel it dry after a shower, then cover it up. Who do I need to impress?

But my mom says my best feature is my smile. And in this picture, it's not there. It's a half-smile, the bare minimum.

I sigh. "Look, I can't fault you for loving him." And even though Sun's my best friend, I really can't. Seth's everything—handsome and sweet, with just enough ambition to make teachers like him. Just goofy enough to endear everyone else to him. "And I can't hate him for loving you, either. I love you both. And obviously the wounds are still fresh, but I'll get over it."

"Whoa. Back up, cowboy." Sun holds up a palm. "Love? That's a little extreme. I don't love him, Isaac. We've been together all of two weeks—*barely* the time you and I were together! You two were what . . . half a year?"

Four months and twenty-three days, actually. Just enough to feel real.

"It's okay to be hurt, Isaac. Seth and I aren't in love. But I do love you, and I don't ever want to be someone who causes you pain. It's not worth it. If it's too much to be around this, just say the word and I'll end it. Okay?"

We've had a similar talk before, and the thing is that I know Sun means every word she says. She really would give Seth up if I asked. And that's why I could never take this from her.

"You know if I wasn't okay, I would tell you," I say.

"You promise?" Sun lifts a pinky.

We lock it in.

"Good," she says. "Wanna split some pumpkin popcorn?"

"Already got him covered." Miranda skips back to us with a bag of orange-tinted popcorn in her hands.

Armand comes back a minute later with a bag of his own. *"What?"* he says, eyeing Miranda's bag. "Isaac and I have been sharing snacks since junior high. I can't eat all this myself."

"Then I'll help you out," Sun says. "Guess I don't have to buy any."

"What about Seth?" Armand says.

"I already told him, he can buy his own."

By the time we do a full lap around the farm, all our collective popcorn has become sort of a free-for-all. We don't really care. It's weird and delicious, and we all have way too much of it until we're too lazy to do much walking, which is the perfect reason to do the hayride.

Honestly, I enjoy the farm. With every picture we take, my smile grows a little bigger. Miranda paints her face to look like a skeleton. Armand buys a book on how to draw dragons. I enjoy schooling Seth on the balloon dart game, which wins me even more popcorn. This time, I give it to him. And by the time the sky turns orange, we're ready for the corn maze.

The maze is harmless and cute during the day, but just before twilight, they let the actors hide, wander, and scare the pants off everyone. This transition is signaled by the Grim Reaper, who strolls over to the corn and guards the entrance to the maze.

"You may en-tah!" The Grim Reaper points his scythe to the path behind him. "But be-wah! For once you en-tah the labyrinth, you may be *forevah* changed."

"Yeah, I'll probably need to change my pants." Seth squeezes Sun's hand. "Do you mind going in before me?"

"My hero," Sun deadpans.

Miranda takes the lead. "You all are chickens."

"The farm chickens have been slaughtah'd by a monstah!" the Grim Reaper says.

I follow Miranda, popcorn in hand. "Good. Otherwise, we wouldn't have a Charlie's Chicken Kitchen in town, now would we?"

"You will *nawt* be laughing long. Mwahha-ha!" The Grim Reaper's fake laugh comes from the throat, and his coughing fit is the last I hear from him as we venture into the maze.

I shouldn't be surprised that the corn maze is pretty tame. This is a family event after all. We follow Armand's suggestion to always make right turns, and I chuckle when I realize some of the corn stalks have been pocked with little Xs. I wonder if anyone has actually found this maze difficult.

At one point, Seth screams bloody murder and all the hairs stand up on my neck. But when we turn around, we find a clown offering him a baby pink balloon. It's not even a demonic clown; it's like a basic, deeply average circus clown with bright frills and everything.

We turn a corner and find a zombie with his mask off, sitting on the ground, checking his phone. "Hey," he says. "Sorry. Gotta catch my breath."

Miranda asks the zombie to take our picture. "Are we almost done?" she asks him. "No offense, but this is kind of . . . tame? And we haven't picked up our pumpkins yet."

The zombie shrugs, apparently unoffended.

"Sure. Turn the corner after the scarecrow and then it's a straight shot to the exit."

"Thanks, mister. Have fun!"

"I won't."

Sun sighs as we turn the corner at the scarecrow. "The worst part is that this corn maze is probably the best scare we can get in Belhaven. We don't even have any good ghost stories in town. Can't we all just pretend that the auditorium at school is haunted?"

"Do you ever go to that thrift shop?" Armand says. "Second Chances? I get some weird vibes from that place."

"Second Ch—" My toe catches on something, throwing my momentum forward. And I'm down. I do a full face plant, chin to soil.

Armand and Miranda rush to help me up, Sun doting while I spit dirt from my mouth. "Oh my gosh! Are you okay?"

"My popcorn . . ." I sulk, my heart in dirty, kernel-sized pieces on the ground.

Armand bursts into laughter. "Of course that's what you're worried about."

Once I'm back on my feet, Seth offers his bag and a little slice of "normal" between us.

But I don't take it. I'm too mesmerized by

what I tripped on.

A pumpkin lies half-buried in the soil. It's not one of those perfect orange pumpkins, either. This one's weird. It's a pale shade of blue—the color reminding me of winter—and it's also tall and thin rather than round and plump. And it's grown in a twisted, tornado sort of pattern.

"Whoa," Seth says. "That's one trippy pumpkin."

"Dollar in the pun jar." Miranda gives Seth a thumbs down.

I take the dark blue stem and heave the pumpkin from the ground, and man, it's heavy. It's not the first one I'd grab for carving, but something about it tugs at me.

"Dibs," I say.

THREE

ISAAC

We wrap up our day at Farmer Elaine's with cider and a stroll around the pumpkin patch where Seth, Sun, Armand, and Miranda each pick the most perfect, spherical, orange, boring pumpkins they can possibly find. Meanwhile, I work on my muscles. My strange, blue, magic pumpkin weighs a ton, and I'm pretty sure my arms are gonna be shaking tomorrow.

"Are you sure you're even allowed to take that one?" Seth asks me. "What if it's a prop? You're gonna steal a prop from the corn maze?"

"I'm gonna pay for it," I say.

"Where do we find another cool one like

that?" Miranda asks. "I've never seen a pumpkin like it. I didn't even know they come in that color."

"What if it's painted?" Sun says.

"I don't think it is." I show her a few little scars on the pumpkin's surface, tiny little scratches. "If it was painted, you should be able to see the orange underneath. Under the blue there's just more blue."

"Shiny blue." And Sun's right. The flesh under the surface shimmers like ice crystals.

Once we've all chosen our pumpkins, we head for the exit. Farmer Elaine still has the same pep and energy she had in the morning, though her crew lolls around yawning and sipping coffee.

"Did y'all find what you were looking for?" she asks. "Adventure and surprises?"

Seth puts his pumpkin on Elaine's table and points to mine. "Surprises, yes. Is he allowed to take that one?"

I set my pumpkin on the table and my arms find sweet relief.

"I don't see why not." Elaine inspects my prize, a big grin spreading across her face. "Ooh, you found a winner, hon! This is a special one."

"How did it get to be like this?" I ask. "I found it in the corn maze."

"Magic." Elaine winks and pops the pumpkin on a scale. "And at thirty cents a pound, this one's gonna cost you five dollars and forty cents, hon. But I'll settle for a photo of you, me, and that gorgeous work of nature. This will be a *hit* on my WowFeed!"

I shrug. "For a free pumpkin? Sweet!"

Elaine hands her phone to Seth. "Sweetie, will you do the honors?"

She gives my pumpkin back and rests a palm on my shoulder, hardcore cheesing for the photo.

"Oh, I hope you don't cut that beauty up," Elaine says. "It's gorgeous. Isn't nature grand?"

Without waiting for a reply, she takes the rest of the group's pumpkins, weighs them, and collects their cash. We're on our way out a few minutes later, once again passing under the witch who wrecked her broom. "Oh, drat! Life can be such a witch!"

We spend the rest of the day at Armand's house, where everyone carves their perfect pumpkins and I busy myself helping them scoop out the spidery guts. I follow Elaine's advice and choose not to carve mine—not necessarily because she asked, but because cutting into it doesn't feel right. I want to preserve it the way it is until it rots away in a week or two.

"Isaac's perfect pumpkin," Seth teases, brandishing his knife. "I say we carve it anyway and give it some character."

I hug the pumpkin close to my chest. "No. Mine."

"It's like your baby now," he says.

"Leave him and his baby alone," Sun says. "Focus and work on your . . . duckling?"

Seth spins his pumpkin around. "It's a basilisk, okay? The serpent king!"

"Why does it have a beak?"

"That's a tongue. See how it splits like that? I'm sure it's not any worse than the rest of yours."

Everyone shows off their designs. Armand carved a beautiful, intricate fire drake, Miranda made a solid vampire, and Sun reveals Peter Pan flying in a starry sky.

"Mine's the best." Seth pouts and sinks into

his chair.

Armand jumps up from his chair. "Hey Isaac, wanna come help me clean up all the pumpkin guts? I wanna toast the seeds."

I follow him into the kitchen and help him rip the seeds from all the stringy goo. I throw them in a strainer and run them under water while Armand preheats the oven.

"How you feeling?" he asks.

I squish some pumpkin goo in my hands and toss it in the trash. "Like this."

Armand nods. "It's gonna get better, you know."

"Yeah," I say. "I know. It's just . . . I don't understand why love has to hurt so much."

Armand takes the strainer from me and spreads the seeds on a baking pan. "I guess I think of love a different way. It's not just that mushy stuff the Thunderlings sing about or that the Disney movies romanticize. It's a lot of things. I haven't experienced the kind that hurts yet. But . . ." He pops the seeds in the oven. "We're young! We don't know half of what we're going to learn about love yet. We probably don't even know ten percent. Isn't that cool to think about?"

I chuckle. "Well, I've had enough dumb life lessons about love for a while."

"Not your call to make, bro," Armand says. "And there's no way to know when life's gonna try to teach us more about it. All I know is you're about to fall in love with these pumpkin seeds, and nothing to get in the way of that."

A slamming sound cuts the air, and I hear someone yell in the living room, "No, Seth. Don't!"

Then comes a gasp, a few seconds of awkward silence, followed by Sun mumbling, "Oh, gosh. You're the worst."

When I get back to the table, my heart drops when I find a knife buried in my pumpkin. Seth's hand hovers over his mouth as if he's holding back a laugh while Miranda and Sun stare daggers at him.

"Seth!" I say. "What the heck, man?"

Seth yanks his knife out and wipes it down with a rag. I rush over and inspect the damage. One deep gash in the side, about an inch long. The cut shimmers in the light, and I run a finger over it.

"I was just giving it payback," Seth says,

"for tripping you. An eye for an eye and all that."

"We tried to stop him," Miranda says.

I know he could've done so much more. I also know it's just a stupid squash. Yet my face suddenly feels hot.

"I told you to leave it alone." My voice shakes.

His grin flips upside down. He puts his hands up as if to shield himself from me, which hurts. It's not like I'm gonna start swinging at him. "Whoa. Don't you think you're overreacting a little bit? I mean . . . it's just a vegetable."

"I know what it is, thanks." My breath quickens and my fists tighten at my sides. "It's not the point. The point is I told you to leave it alone, and you cut into it anyway. I mean, *an eye for an eye and all that*? Really? Do you even care about anyone besides yourself?"

"Dang, man. I didn't realize you were gonna flip out. I'm sorry. I'll buy you another one."

"Do you understand that you ripped my heart out of my chest and stomped on it?" I want to take the words back as soon as they fall out, but I'm on a slippery slope.

Seth picks up the pumpkin scoop and fidgets. "We're not actually talking about the pumpkin, are we?"

Miranda taps Sun on the shoulder and points to the front door. "Come on. Let's get some air."

Sun casts us a worried glance, but I see Armand nod at her from the kitchen. He doesn't say anything, but he doesn't leave, either. Miranda and Sun slip on their jackets and slide out the door.

Seth sighs and stares down at his lap. "Isaac, I thought we agreed not to make this weird."

"Don't put this on me. It's *been* weird," I say. "Flirting with me in the car while you had your arms around my best friend? And I'm supposed to just act like it's not happening."

Seth narrows his eyes. "Flirting? How?"

"Your 'don't leave me' talk and your 'let's share popcorn' and all that. With all this history between us, that hurt."

Seth keeps fidgeting with the scoop. "You think I'm not hurting, too?"

"Why would you be hurting? You're the one who ended things. You said you needed time to work on you or whatever, and then a few days later you started dating my best friend. Was that time between us even real? Is what you have with Sun real?"

"Yes," Seth says, "it's both. And, Isaac, bisexuality is real, you know. I didn't break up with you because I stopped having feelings for you, or guys in general. I broke up with you because we're not compatible. I can still like you and recognize that things weren't working."

Now it's my turn to be quiet. My brain zooms in on this statement. "What do you mean?"

Seth puts down the scoop and finally looks me in the eye. "I mean, for starters, our interests are all over the place. You never want to come to sports things or do any outdoor stuff with me unless the whole group is there. And honestly, I'm just not that into video games."

"That was the deal breaker?" I ask. "But Sun doesn't love sports, either."

"No. It's not just one thing. It's all the little things. We live in two different worlds. Your whole family is cool with you being gay, and mine's been kind of weird with me these past four months."

We've talked about this before. Coming out is a different experience for everybody. Sometimes it feels more like peeling back a curtain than walking out of a closet, revealing ourselves an inch at a time and hoping the world will welcome us. And I almost wonder if Seth is snapping his curtain shut again.

"So, you broke up with me because you're embarrassed," I say slowly. "That's messed up. Is that what it is?"

"Isaac, it's complicated." Seth sighs. "What happened between us isn't as simple as one thing or another. It's everything, and it's not easy to put into words. You're an awesome guy. You're good-looking. Kind. Probably going to a good college someday. How could I not have feelings for you?" His voice breaks, and it's the first time I've seen him show any kind of emotion about our breakup.

In a petty way, it kind of makes me happy, but it also stings.

"It's just not simple," he continues. "I don't know how to put it all into words. You deserve better."

I run my thumb over the new scar in the pumpkin, tears stinging my eyes. In the grand scheme of things, I don't actually care about the pumpkin or the fact that Seth decided to stab it for no reason. It's the things *I* don't know how to put into words. All I know is that my heart is hurting so much that I've caused a whole scene amongst my best friends, and I've ruined what could've been a perfect day.

If only Seth and I had never been a thing—never met, for that matter.

If only I hadn't let my guard down so fully.

If only, if only, if only . . ..

"I probably shouldn't be around you for a while." When I say this, I know what I'm giving up—this core group of five and everything that ties it together. I stand and pick up my pumpkin.

"Maybe some space is good," Seth says. "For me, too."

Armand stops pretending that he isn't listening and grabs his keys. "Do you need a ride home, Isaac?"

I shake my head. "I'm gonna walk. Clear my head."

That's the beauty of Belhaven. The town is walkable enough that I'll be home in less than twenty minutes.

"Me, too," Seth says.

"I'm gonna offer Sun and Miranda a ride." Armand walks me to the door and pats me on the shoulder.

I go for an awkward, armless hug while I carry my wounded pumpkin. "Thanks for today, and . . . sorry about everything."

"You're okay," Armand says. "Some things take time and space. If you ever wanna talk or anything, I'm here."

Before I get to the door, I hear Miranda and Sun on the front steps, Miranda speaking in low, intense tones.

"You shouldn't have said yes to Seth! Now the Fall Ball is probably going to be weird, if we're still even going."

"I know," Sun says sadly. "Isaac promised me he'd be okay with it."

"You're supposed to know him better than that," Miranda says.

"And sacrifice my own happiness? I can't make all my decisions based on Isaac. I would've told him the same thing."

"Well, you should've given him time to heal."

Armand opens the door, and Sun and Miranda stop talking. Sun rubs her elbows as if she's cold.

"I'm sorry," I tell them, "for all the awkwardness."

Miranda excuses everything and insists that everything's okay, but Sun doesn't look me in the eye. I can tell she's upset.

"We have more talking to do," Sun says. "You told me you were okay."

"I just need space."

I set out for home, and Armand calls out from the doorframe, "Text me when you make it home."

"You're just letting him walk?" Miranda whispers, and it's the last I hear from them before I'm out of earshot.

That's how I know I've really ruined the night. There's so much tension in the air that now all my friends are getting mad at each other, too. And this is a me thing. I own it.

In my head, I sing a Vegas Thunderlings song. *You're a cursed man. Everything you touch turns to ash.*

The walk home is quiet. Some folks are out walking their dogs or shooting hoops in their driveways. I cross paths with an old lady in a jumpsuit who's out powerwalking with a pedometer. "Ooh, nice pumpkin!" she tells me.

I give her a little half-smile. The chipper old lady and the satisfying crunch of leaves under my boots isn't quite enough to life my spirits. I'm pretty sure only a good night's sleep will do that now, but I haven't even started my weekend homework. It's going to be a long night.

When I make it home, Mom and Dad are cozied up on the couch watching some true crime doc—at least, that's what I assume by all the screaming going on.

"Hi, mijo," Mom says. "I didn't hear the car. Did Armand drive you home?"

"He did," I lie.

"Oh, I didn't see the headlights. I must be getting sucked into this reality show again. Is that your pumpkin?"

I hold it out for Mom and Dad to see. "Weird, huh?"

Mom makes an *ahh* sound.

Dad wrinkles his brows. "You sure that's not radioactive? You're not gonna turn into

Pumpkin Man, are you? We need to make *calabacitas* out of you? Go get some corn, some cheese?"

"Ha. That's great, Dad," I deadpan, heading for the stairs to my bedroom. "You already have all the cheese."

"Wait, mijo, did you have fun?" Mom asks. "How was it with Seth being there?"

I freeze with one foot on the staircase. "Ma . . . I don't want to talk about Seth anymore. Okay?"

Without another word, I head for my bedroom and shut the door behind me. I slump down until my butt's on the ground and I'm cradling my pumpkin on my knees. I shut my eyes and let out a deep breath, reorienting myself in my little corner of the world. Chris D'Agosto posters, small TV, an overly organized desk where all the homework I need to do is piled in a crisp stack of papers . . ..

I slink back up the wall and carry my pumpkin to the dresser by my window.

"What a day, huh?" I run my thumb over the slit again. "And to top it all off, I'm talking to a pumpkin. This is my life now."

I nod to myself.

I kick off my shoes and my phone buzzes in my pocket.

Yo, you make it home yet?

I drop onto my bed and let my phone lie on my chest for a minute.

"Yeah, Armand," I mutter to myself, "I made it home."

I know my friends care; I know my family loves me.

So why do I feel so alone lately? So out of place? Like a pumpkin in a corn maze.

I look to my strange find. "So, what's your story, huh?"

I'm bewildered when a flash of light ripples through my room, so bright I have to throw my arms up and cover my eyes.

"What the . . .."

When I uncover my face, my pumpkin has sprouted a pair of legs. Male legs in trousers and dusty leather boots stick out where the bottom should be. They stand on my dresser, and the stem of the pumpkin is almost to my ceiling.

I drop my phone. "*What the—!*"

The legs take a step and tumble off my

dresser, propelling the pumpkin into my lap before a pair of arms burst from the sides. The gloved hands flail around, find me, and tap my shoulder. They find my elbows, then my neck, then my face. Two fingers go in my mouth and tug at the corners of my lips. My heart responds with a leap against my rib cage. Seth was right to stab this crazy spider pumpkin. I yelp and shove the walking vegetable off my lap, and all the pumpkin flesh disappears.

Where the squash used to be, a teenage boy in a prince costume tumbles to the floor.

FOUR

JACK

It's only day two of my curse, and I've already gone completely mental. Gone are the corn stalks and starry night sky. Instead, I'm in a boxy room, locking eyes with a boy I've never seen before. His eyes are as round as the blood moon, and for a second, I fear he might scream.

"*Youwereinthepumpkin,*" he says in one breath.

I scoot away from him and massage my back. A fall to the ground is a nasty way to wake up. "And who are you?" I ask. "Are you an ally of the Winter Queen? Have I solved the corn labyrinth? No . . . this is still the curse. *Madness.* I've met the Gray Lady and forgotten her face. This is death. Oh, stars and gods!"

"You were in the pumpkin," the boy repeats.

"Pumpkin?" I ask. "What pumpkin?"

The boy stands and massages his head, pacing back and forth. "Dad was right. It was radioactive. I'm sick. I'm losing my mind. I'm inventing people in my head now." He stops, looks me up and down, and taps my chest. "Ah! You have texture. Detail. I'm *really* sick. I've hallucinated Prince Charming."

I dig my hands into my hair, baring my teeth. "My name is *not* Prince Charming. I'm Prince Jack of the Kingdom of Veron! Now, tell me why I'm here. Am I your prisoner? Are you cursed, too?"

"I'm obviously cursed by something." The boy sits back on his bed and cradles his temples again. "This is not normal. This is not normal at all."

Something taps on the door. "Mijo?" a woman calls. She sounds nothing like Nev. She sounds kind.

I wonder if that's the boy's name. Instinctively, I reach for the doorknob. I want to explore the castle and get some answers.

But the boy slaps my hand, opens a different

door, and shoves me into a dark room full of strange clothes. "Stay in there and shut up."

"I'm not your prisoner," I growl as he seals me into the abyss. I press my ear to the door and listen to what's happening on the other side. The boy speaks to a woman.

"Is everything okay, mijo? You're acting really strange tonight, and I just heard you yelling and throwing stuff on the floor. What's going on?"

"I'm okay, Mom. I'm sorry. Just had to vent for a bit, but hey, I punched a pillow, and now I'm gonna put on some music and everything will be all good by morning. Promise."

"Hm. Okay. Don't make me take your door away. Last warning. Because I care about you."

"Got it, Ma."

"All right . . . love you, okay?"

"Love you, too."

Love. The word is an arrow to my chest. Under my tunic, something stings. I touch my hand to my chest and my glove comes away wet.

When the boy opens the door, light floods into the tiny prison he shoved me in. He puts a finger to his lips. "We need to be quiet so that doesn't happen again." He gasps and promptly raises his voice again. "Oh man, you're bleeding."

My face goes cold at the sight of my crimson-stained gloves. What sorcery does this boy wield that turns words into piercing weapons? I undo the top buttons on my tunic, exposing a thin scratch about the length of my thumb. Blood doesn't spill from it, but the thin red line rattles my nerves. "Your words are daggers," I gasp. "You *are* an ally of Nev."

When he sees the cut, all the color spills from the boy's face. "The knife," he whispers. "Um, I'm gonna get you cleaned up."

"Your words are daggers, mijo." I roll over and bury my face in something soft and plushy. "Oh, stars and gods," I moan.

The boy reaches up and pulls on a thin chain, filling the tiny room with light. "My name is not mijo, it's Isaac." He steps over me and fumbles through his belongings. "Where's my first aid kit? Ah! Got it."

Isaac takes a knee and opens a big white box. "How is this happening?" he asks. "You were in the pumpkin. My friend cut into that pumpkin earlier, and your cut looks exactly like the place where he stabbed it. I'm not sure how you did that. Halloween effects aren't *that* good." He pauses. "Wait a minute . . .. *Of course.* This is all a Halloween prank. Right? Who put you up to this?"

There's that phrase again. *Hollow Wene.*

"I'm not a prank," I say. "I'm a prince. I don't know what you're babbling on about with this pumpkin. I've been cursed by Nev, the Winter Queen. Seven days in the worst place. This is my second day."

Isaac twists open a brown bottle and rips into a paper strip. "Uh-huh. Cool backstory, bro. You've got the royal look down. How much did you pay for that costume?"

I study my ruffled sleeves. "I paid nothing. This was made for me. What's Hollow Wene?"

Isaac rolls his eyes as he pours potion onto a ball of cotton. "Pointless. Here comes the sting—sorry."

The ball of cotton comes down on my wound, and it's like a black flame to my chest. I grit my teeth and suck in a lungful of air. "What infernal potion is this?"

"Alcohol," Isaac says. "You're what? Fifteen? Sixteen? All these years and you've never had to get cleaned up with this stuff? This is a childhood staple." He scrubs the liquid fire on me, searing my soul. When I can't take it anymore, a calming tingling sensation trickles over the wound and Isaac covers it with a sticky patch.

I peel off a glove and touch the patch. It's porous and gummy and strange, and I start to peel it off right away. "And what sorcery is *this*?"

"Bandage," Isaac says. "Stop touching it. You don't want to get infected. How do you not know this?"

I button my tunic. "In my kingdom, alcohol is only for turning men and women into fools, not for healing wounds. But stars and gods, I do feel much better. Are you a nurse? Or a magician?"

"Nope. Just a boy." Isaac tumbles onto his bed and stares at the ceiling. "If I were a magician, I'd make some people disappear. And if I were a nurse, I'd start working on my messed-up head."

"You want people to disappear? What's wrong with your head?"

"Oh, I'm just having vivid hallucinations

of pumpkin boys who don't understand bandages and ask a million questions. Something like that." Isaac grabs a pillow and hugs it to his chest. "I'm just hurting."

I pick up the brown bottle Isaac used to heal me and shake the liquid. "Do you need the alcohol potion?"

"Not that kind of hurt, man. You know . . . heartbreak?"

Heartbreak. The first time I ever heard the term from Samuel, I was so alarmed. "Shouldn't that kill you?" I had asked him.

And Samuel had said, "Sometimes it does. It almost always feels like it can. I suppose that's why we need songs and stories. They help us know we're not alone."

I crawl out of the tiny prison and scoot up next to Isaac's bed. While I don't know this boy, I certainly don't want him to die from heartbreak. Samuel didn't train me to fix anyone's head or hallucinations, but I owe this boy for fixing me up.

"Sir Isaac," I say, "my mentor always taught me that stories were good for broken hearts. I don't remember many stories that were taught to me, but now that I'm cursed, I suppose I have a story of my own. I just don't know the ending yet. Would you like to hear what happened to me?"

Isaac rubs his eyes. "You're a hallucination, and I have to do my homework." He stands and walks to a strange contraption with a glowing screen. "If you're still real tomorrow, you can tell me then."

"Oh." I look around the room, feeling out of place. I cleared the labyrinth. Now what do I do? "Should I leave?"

"Don't go outside that door. I wouldn't know how to explain you to my parents." Isaac messes with his contraption. "Just sit there and be quiet. I'm sure you'll disappear soon enough."

Rich music pours from Isaac's machine. It's like nothing I've ever heard before, energizing and full.

You're a cursed man, the lyrics declare. *Everything you touch turns to ash.*

My heart skips a beat. An invisible orchestra is playing my story.

I listen, studying the moonlight on Isaac's window. I've lost a full day. I remember turning blue and undergoing a strange transformation, and then nothing. My brain skipped straight to a few moments ago, falling to the floor and feeling as though I'd been stuffed in a box. The whole time, I didn't dream or feel anything.

But I do feel now. It occurs to me that maybe my own heart is broken. That in my banishment from Veron, I'm alone. That even though I'm not trapped in a corn labyrinth, I'm still lost.

So, as the invisible orchestra plays, I tell my story to myself.

FIVE

JACK

Growing up, I knew of two kingdoms—Veron, The Summer Kingdom, and Invera, The Winter Kingdom. They aren't divided by ocean, valley, or wall—just a thin, invisible curtain of magic where the sun ends and the snow begins. Samuel used to show me maps of the ages. In the earliest times, long before my great-great-grandparents, there were actually four realms. Then war broke out, and Invera consumed the other lands one by one until it covered most of the map.

My late grandparents were the ones to end the war, working with late King of Invera to negotiate peace before Invera could swallow us, too. Now Veron has one corner of the land

and some of the sea.

The terms were simple enough—no one could cross the boundary uninvited. We would never know the mysteries of frost, and the Inverans would never know the kiss of the golden sun. And for many years, that was called peace.

I grew up knowing I should never touch the snow, though my parents didn't necessarily trust me not to. That's why Samuel would accompany me to the forest. There, I would sit on a rock and marvel at the chilled wonderland on the other side of the curtain. On our side, we enjoyed crisp green grass and thick, full trees. On the other, thick blankets of snow and barren branches, all divided by a thread. Sometimes I'd put my finger all the way up to the edge, almost daring myself to cross over.

"What's it like?" I asked Samuel.

"I've never experienced it," Samuel said. "And those who know it have never been allowed to return to Veron. What do you think it's like?"

I watched a deer bound over a hill, clumps of snow springing up under its feet. "Soft," I murmured, "like clouds or cotton. Why can't I ever touch?"

Samuel sighed. "I'm afraid the grass is always greener on the other side of the fence."

"But all I see is white."

"No, Jack. It's an expression. It means you always want the thing you can't have. If you cross that curtain, you can't come back. Then you'll see how green our grass really is, and it's all you'll ever want. The snow belongs to Invera; the sun belongs to us. It's just the way it is."

"Why can't everything belong to all of us?"

"Because it's the rules."

I hated the rules. I would've given anything for them to change.

And on my sixteenth birthday, they did.

We sat at dinner, and my father cleared his throat. "An announcement!" he said. "Friends. Family. We have negotiated new terms with Nev, Queen of Invera. It is time for a change. Soon you will all be able to cross over the curtain any time you want, and the citizens of the Winter Kingdom will finally be able to enjoy the sun."

"A joyous day is on the horizon." My

mother set her goblet down, folded her hands, and gave me the biggest smile I'd ever seen from her. "Jack. You, my son, are soon to be wed to Princess Aurora of Invera. Your union will join our houses forever and expand our lovely dominion. Veron and Invera are to be one!"

Everyone at the banquet table started clapping, except for Samuel. There was something in his face I couldn't quite define. I saw their hands move, but I barely heard them. It was like my ears were plugged.

I swallowed my bite of turkey leg, half-chewed, with an audible gulp. "*Marriage*?" I breathed.

It's never been unusual for Veron royals to marry as young as sixteen, and for their marriages to be arranged. I had always known this was coming, but the news was still enough of a shock to knock the wind out of my lungs.

"Oh, he's choked up!" Hilda, the cook, clapped her hands, her cheeks rosy and full. "That's so very sweet. I just love love. And oh, how I can't wait to experience snow."

"Marriage," I repeated.

"Yes," my father said. "My time as king will soon end. You must rise to your responsibilities, and that means preparing to carry the bloodline so Veron may prosper for another generation. You'll be a fine king, and a perfect husband for Princess Aurora."

"She really is radiant," my mother gushed. "She's certain to be enamored of you, too. And most importantly, you'll produce a strong heir to the Seat."

My knee jittered under the table, my boot heel knocking on our floor. Suddenly, even my orange potatoes didn't look so appealing. *Heirs? Wives? Seat?* "But I've never met the princess."

The joy on Hilda's face melted away.

"Why, you never needed to, dear," my mother said. "You can take our word for it. You'll see her on your wedding day. Samuel will prepare you accordingly. He's instructed you beautifully in the ways of the sword and all you need to know for your formal education. Now, we must guide you to the altar. We'll get you fitted to look as dashing as possible, and if I may be candid, Samuel needs to remind you how to shine your boots and fix your hair. You also need to be prepared for winter."

I looked down the table at Samuel again, giving him an expression that clearly said, *Help me.* But he didn't look back; instead, he stared at his plate, his dinner untouched.

I pushed my supper away from me. "May I be excused?"

My father wrinkled his brows. "Jack, I should think you'd be grateful for winter. You've hardly spoken of anything else since boyhood."

"And now he's so excited, he can barely contain himself." Hilda beamed.

"I need to collect my emotions." I tossed my napkin over my plate and stalked out of the dining hall.

Sulking on the castle grounds, I skipped stones on a pond, half trying to hit a duck. *My family just sold my future.* I launched another stone.

I'm betrothed to someone I don't know. Another stone.

Nobody asked me how I feel about this. I swung the next stone so hard, my shoulder popped.

I didn't ask them for this! I stood, picked up

a boulder as large as my head, and raised it.

And Samuel crept up behind me and snatched the rock out of my hands before I could throw it. He dropped the rock, grabbed my wrist, and glared at me, his grip like iron.

"Have a seat, *Your Majesty*." Samuel's tone was like gravel. "I ought to toss you into this pond."

When he released my arm, we sat together.

"Samuel," I said, "why is this happening? And why are you so upset?"

"You need to tread lightly," Samuel said. "I've been watching our new *Winter Queen*, Nev. If she suspects you are anything but elated about your upcoming marriage to her daughter, she will not make your life easy." I'd never seen him look so grave, his eyes wide and piercing.

Something about his words made me dizzy. "You've been visiting Invera? But it's forbidden. It's dangerous. What if you never came back?"

"I had to know what we were facing," Samuel said. "From the start, I didn't agree with the new deal. The king and queen think they're doing what's best for the people, but Nev wants to put Veron under her cold thumb and manage your rule herself. This was all about her from the start. She's been waiting for just the right moment to fulfill the unfinished designs of her ancestors— eternal winter everywhere. And it's not all fluffy and soft, Isaac. It's inhospitable to life. A little bit is a temporary joy. Eternal winter is death. We might as well march right up to the Gray Lady's door."

My lungs turned to fire, my breaths short and hot. "But Invera and Veron have peace! It's been written."

"Because Nev is playing the long game, and she has been all along." Samuel pulled his knees up to his chest and stared at the horizon. "I've tried to reason with your parents already. They won't have it. The only thing I can think of is for you to take her down from within the joined houses. When your union with Aurora is official, our protection against the Winter Queen will fracture . . . unless you can master Summer's Glow in time for her attack."

I picked up another stone, and Samuel lowered my hand.

"Stars and gods," I said, "I thought Summer's Glow was a myth."

"It may be our last hope." Samuel snatched the stone from me and used it to doodle four quadrants on the ground. "Invera overtook the kingdoms of old because Invera had an ancient magic called Winter's Bite. Rival magics were lost over time— Autumn's Breath, Spring's Waters, and Summer's Glow." As he spoke, Samuel drew in the quadrants. A snowflake. A gust of wind. A raindrop. A sun. "They exist, Isaac. Nev knows this because she has mastered Winter's Bite. She intends to join our houses so she can snuff out the remaining warmth in the land. But Nev would never expect you to master the Glow. You can turn the tides against her."

This was what I called a *fairy tale.* A bedtime story. To cure heartbreak and all that.

I had only heard two other details about Summer's Glow—that it had been lost generations ago, and . . ..

"Isn't that only possible through an act of true love?" I asked.

Samuel put his head to his knees and pulled them closer to his chest. "Yes."

I didn't have to speak my next question aloud. *What if I never fall in love with Princess Aurora?* I'd never even kissed a girl before.

"What is she like, Samuel?" I asked. "In all the time you've been spying on Nev, you must have seen Aurora, right?"

"Yes," Samuel said. "She doesn't possess the same shadow as her mother. She's beautiful. Sweet. Kind." In spite of all this, he looked sad, his voice heavy. He stood and scrubbed away his rock drawing with the heel of his boot. "But if I may be so bold, I don't think you and Princess Aurora are meant to fall in love. We may have to fight Nev the hard way."

"What do you mean?" I asked.

"I know you better than anyone. Perhaps better than you know yourself." And with that comment, Samuel started to walk away. "Happy birthday, Jack."

I stood. "Samuel?"

"Remember to tread lightly." Samuel didn't look back. "We'll keep training tomorrow. Harder than ever. I expect the Winter Queen will attempt to curse you."

Curse me, I thought. Training was supposed

to be a formality, a precaution in case darkness ever crossed the land. I never expected I'd actually need to learn anything.

Maybe I'd at least find the curse exciting.

The next day was business as usual with Samuel. Swords. Curse defense. Boot shining and hair care. I kept asking him what he meant when he said Aurora and I weren't meant to fall in love, but he always changed the subject. This went on every day.

Until the day of the wedding, when I saw Aurora for the first time.

Samuel was right, and for that matter, so were my parents. Aurora was lovely. I'd never seen an Inveran in person before. Like many of the guests, Aurora had a long shock of silky white hair that reached all the way down to her waist. Her ears were pointed, and her eyes were a stunning shade of violet, like a twilight sky. And like the stars, she had a gorgeous smattering of light freckles across the bridge of her nose.

I took Aurora's wrist and kissed the back of her hand, which wasn't as cold as I'd been expecting. "It's lovely to meet you, Princess."

Aurora curtseyed, her voice feather-light.

"And you as well, my prince."

Queen Nev watched the interaction with a look that chilled me to the bone. Somehow, Aurora was a perfect copy of Nev, yet not at all the same. In Aurora, I saw kindness. In Nev's ageless features, I saw the end of the world. Her hair was gathered into a tight, silver bun, and gold snowflake ornaments dangled from the rods that held it together. Nev crossed the room and took my chin in her hands.

When her fingers grazed me, I saw my breath leave my body in an icy cloud. A shiver raced down my back.

So this is winter.

"Soft eyes. Thick, gorgeous hair." The Winter Queen turned my head to the side. "Strong jaw. You are just as handsome as I've been promised." She let go of my chin and tapped my chest with a sharp, pale blue fingernail. "Her heart will be well-guarded with you, I trust. Now come, Aurora. Let's get you ready."

Aurora flashed me a weak smile. Her mother spun her around and ushered her away with a team of stylists and maids.

Samuel stole my last moment of quiet, leaning in to whisper in my ear, "And?"

One word. Three letters. Only I knew everything they contained. "I don't know yet, Samuel," I whispered back.

"I've never believed in love at first sight myself," he said. "It's a fable. Give it time."

And the rest of the day sped up in a blur. I couldn't count the men and women fussing over me, bathing me as if I had never learned to clean myself, feeding me tiny morsels of cheese and fruit as to keep my energy up— but not spoil my appetite—stuffing me into shimmering garb, complaining that I'd lost some weight, stripping me down to make adjustments to my suit and then stuffing me into it once again, styling my hair this way and then that way until nobody disagreed anymore, polishing my crown, shining my boots, offering me marriage advice, offering me *parenting* advice, and during small breaks, rewriting and practicing vows with me.

The whole time, I was a duck on the pond, floating while everyone else knocked me around and prepared me for the wedding. Or perhaps I was a roasted pig being prepped for dinner. All I could think about was this sense of impending doom—of Nev towering over me until she was ready to toss me aside and spray my world with frosted graves. I'd only known Aurora for a few hours, but I knew she deserved better. Maybe she *would* fare better marrying into my family, but I still wouldn't be what she deserved.

Because as I stood at the altar with her at sundown, an enchanted snowfall melting onto her crisp blue veil, I only had one thought:

That even though Aurora was lovely, our marriage would never be worthy of Summer's Glow.

"Does His Majesty, Prince Jack Zuka, take Her Majesty, Aurora Frost, to be his lovely wife for as long as you both shall live, in summers and winters, 'til death do you part?"

Just say the words, my brain urged me. The silence fell around me thicker than blankets of snow, hundreds of eyes drilling into me but none so sharp as Nev's cold gaze.

Say it now, my brain urged.

My tongue felt like cotton.

"I can't," I whispered.

A collective gasp rolled through the crowd.

Aurora nodded at me, her expression unflinching.

Samuel narrowed his eyes, chin to fists and elbows on his knees.

"Come again?" the priest asked.

"I can't," I repeated.

"*I beg your pardon!*" The Winter Queen swept up the marble steps, a storm of white fuzz and silver satin trailing behind her. Before I could breathe, her fingers were on my chin again. "What did you just say?"

I stared Nev in the eyes. "I can't marry your daughter. I'm sorry." I pulled away from her grip and took Aurora's hand. "Aurora, you're lovely. Any man would be lucky to have you as his princess . . . but I can't do this."

Aurora gave me that nod again, a light smile nudging the corners of her lips. "I understand, Prince Jack. I saw you in a dream, and while our destinies are intertwined, our love is not fated. We must not force Lady Fortune's hand."

Nev rounded on her daughter and dug a nail into her collarbone. "Yes, we must. Oh, you selfish girl, this was never about you, or this stupid boy. This is about the good people of Invera and Veron uniting as one! Experiencing the pleasures of summer and winter as a shared people! Look at them, daughter." The Winter Queen gestured into the crowd of stunned faces. In that crowd, I found my father staring at his toes and my mother holding onto her pearls. "This union is what they want. You would deny them a lifetime of happiness?" She turned back to me. "You would deny my daughter a *child*?"

I swallowed a lump in my throat, realizing I was still holding Aurora's hand. "That's not it. I want to serve the people in a way of my choosing. We can find a way."

The priest closed his book and took a large, awkward step back.

Nev laughed. "Hm. I see. Prince Jack thinks he can do better than my daughter. Then I'll give you plenty of time to think, Your Majesty. Seven days, in fact. Seven cursed days in the worst place imaginable. We'll see how you feel at the end of that time . . . if you return."

The Winter Queen rolled up her furry sleeves.

Aurora tightened her grasp on my hand.

"Mother, what are you doing?"

Nev spread her arms apart and an orange light appeared in her palms, like a tiny sun.

"No!" Samuel leapt from his seat and charged toward the altar, his sword raised above his head. A pair of brutish men rose from the front row and restrained him. "Unhand me, you heathens!" He called over his shoulder and into the crowd, "What are you all doing? Fight for your prince!"

Aurora let go of my hand, then threw herself in front of me. "No, Mother."

As a tingle spread down my body, I spent the last of my energy trying to push Aurora out of Nev's path. I had no idea what was coming—only that it wouldn't be good. Perhaps all my training with Samuel had prepared me. After all, we'd brainstormed a thousand dreadful curses.

Vinecrawler?

Dragon?

Loss of all my senses?

No, reality is always stranger.

I suppose the Winter Queen turned me into a pumpkin.

MONDAY, OCTOBER 27
THE CURSE OF THE DRAGON SLAYER

SIX

ISAAC

I wake up in last night's clothes, my face in my arms and one headphone nestled in my ear. Somehow, I fell asleep at my desk, my homework half-finished and my phone off the charger. The first thing I do is turn around to check on the *prince.*

He's gone, and the blue pumpkin has returned. It's not on my dresser where I last saw it in squash-form. It's now tucked against my pillow with my sheets draped over the bottom half. Like I was trying to play a prank on my parents and tucked a vegetable into bed so I could sneak out at night, or some other ridiculous thing.

I rub the sleep from my eyes and rush to

uncover the pumpkin.

It's armless. Legless. Faceless.

It's just a weird blue pumpkin again.

"There's no way I dreamed in that much detail," I mutter. As much as I didn't believe in him, Prince Jack seemed so vividly real. I heard him hit the floor when he transformed, and so did my mom. I saw the blood on his tunic. I felt his muscles tense when I cleaned him up.

When I roll the pumpkin over, a bandage clings to the surface.

Apparently, I hallucinated so strongly that I had bandaged a pumpkin and put it to bed.

It's like your baby, Seth had said. Oh, how my blood had boiled when he stabbed the pumpkin.

Seth. Gosh, there's still *all that* to work out. Friend drama. Ex drama. I really made a mess of things last night.

I'm afraid to peel off the bandage, but I do it anyway, and now things are even weirder. There's still a gash where Seth stabbed the vegetable, but it doesn't go all the way through. It's just a little scar, like somebody ran a toothpick over it. And I know that part of the night was real. Everything up until I got home was real, right?

Honestly, I have no idea.

There's dry blood on the bandage, a patch of copper brown. There's blood on the bandage but not on the pumpkin.

And it can't be my blood. I don't have any wounds. Where else would the blood have come from?

My eyes go to the floor.

"Boots," I say suspiciously.

I feel like a detective gathering clues. There's a pair of black boots on the ground and one brown glove, the faint new-leather scent filling my room. As an experiment, I step into the boots and walk around my bed. It's like trudging through water, and there's way too much space for my toes. Then I line one boot up next to my Vans and guess there's probably a difference of two or three sizes. These are not my boots, and that is not my glove.

I pool all the evidence together on my bed—boots, glove, pumpkin, bandage.

If I had yarn and some pins, I'd be stringing a web all over my room cooking up conspiracy theories. So far, all I've ruled out is a black-out trip to a costume shop, and only because the accessories aren't my size. I'm eighty percent confident the prince was real, but why am I left with this pumpkin again?

Where does all this leave me?

My laptop produces a trio of chirps that mean biology class is starting soon.

Late for school!

Without changing clothes, I stumble into my Vans. I throw the sheets over my "evidence," run a quick comb through my hair and some mouthwash through my teeth, and I book it out of my house and run like the wind.

Mom and Dad both leave the house way before I do every morning—Mom for her shift at the hospital and Dad to open the bakery. Therefore, nobody ever wakes me, but I'm pretty sure if my mom finds out I'm late for school, she'll start getting me up at four-thirty. And I just can't deal with that nonsense.

I rush through the front gates of Belhaven High about twelve minutes later, sweaty and breathless. Of course, the security guard stops me on his golf cart with the little dragon sticker on the bumper. Fun fact: the guard's son plays our mascot, Boomer the Belhaven

Dragon, which looks a lot more like a fuzzy gecko. Worst school mascot ever. "School ID?"

I sigh and dig my card out of my wallet.

"You're late," the guard tells me.

"I noticed."

The guard hands me back my ID. "Go sign in at the registrar first. You need a pass."

My conversation with the registrar isn't any different. She tells me I'm late, and I tell her that I noticed. She writes me a pass to biology.

On my way to class, I pass about fifty million flyers advertising the Fall Ball on Friday—Halloween night. According to the Count Chocula knock-off digitized into every flyer, the Fall Ball will be sponsored by the student "count-sil". This same vampire also reminds us to wear a school-appropriate costume and to bring three dollars or a donation of canned food—or blood. I groan to myself. Student council had way too much fun thinking about these flyers. This is the first year Belhaven High is trying a school dance on Halloween. Dad was at the last PTA meeting, and he says it's all about keeping us out of trouble or whatever.

For the past month or so, we were all talking about going as a group—*we* meaning me, Armand, Miranda, Sun, and Seth. In a small town like Belhaven, there's not really much else to do on Halloween. Again, no good ghost stories. The kids go get their candy. The fire department puts on a mediocre haunted house. Farmer Elaine's stays open. The Fall Ball sounded like the best way to spend Halloween, only now I'm not so sure I'm going anymore. My parents and friends will insist I do, and I don't really have a better alternative. I also don't have a costume yet, but maybe I can stay home and be an old man giving out candy.

Or better yet, I could turn out the lights, pretend not to be home, and watch *Hocus Pocus* while *I* eat all the candy.

Yes. This is a thing.

I get to biology, and the first thing I see is that everyone's already partnered up to dissect frogs.

Mrs. McKelvey gives me a maternal look. "You're late, Mr. Costa."

I don't tell her I noticed because I actually like Mrs. McKelvey.

I hand her my pass from the registrar. "I'm really sorry."

"Everything well?"

"Yeah," I say. "Just a rough night."

"We've all been there. Well, you can go work with Charlinda and Martel. You'll be our group of three today." While Charlinda and Martel wave at me from the back of the room, Mrs. McKelvey passes me a bio worksheet where we're supposed to record weights and measurements and answer a bunch of questions about frog parts. Normally I *love* dissections, but Charlinda and Martel are pros at this and I'm not feeling very coordinated today. So we make a deal. I'll do the academic heavy lifting and let them play with the frog.

Weirdly though, throughout the whole lab session, my mind keeps wandering to that Frog Prince story. The one where the princess kisses a bunch of frogs or whatever. I find myself looking at the world a little differently. Like what if every frog and every bird and every pumpkin has a story that's way more complicated than we've ever suspected? I have a pumpkin in my room that I swear turned into a prince for at least an hour.

So, I look at that poor amphibian who croaked a long time ago, flat on its back with its legs all long and limp, and I wonder: What if we're actually carving into some cursed royal or something? And there are twelve other frogs just like this all over the lab.

What are we *doing*?

Without warning, my stomach lurches. Full twist. I drop my pencil and clutch my gut. "Oh, man."

Martel claps a hand on my shoulder. "You good, man?"

I hold up a pointer finger and turn away, fighting for control of my stomach. A deep breath in. A cleansing thought—babbling brooks . . . puffy clouds.

I dash out of the lab and bolt for the nearest restroom, ready to puke up my entire life.

Mrs. McKelvey pokes her head out the door. "Sweetie, your hall pass! Mr. Costa! Mr. Costa!"

A hall monitor paces around like a caged tiger, and bless Mrs. McKelvey, because as soon as he makes a beeline for me, she rushes to my defense. "Just let him go, Eric. He's with me right now."

My next classes are no easier.

Every time Mr. Becker asks us to "solve for x" in Algebra, I'm sitting there trying to solve my ex. When Mrs. Cruze-Silva takes us through the twisted mind of Edgar Allen Poe, my brain does tireless mental gymnastics. It somersaults from Poe to creepy, backflips to Halloween, cartwheels to pumpkins, and when it finally lands on princes, I wonder if I've gone as mad as the speaker in the poem. At least Mrs. Cruze-Silva is cool. She goes all out with Poe. Lights out. Sheet over her head and flashlight under her chin. Goofy voices.

By the time lunch hits, I'm *starving*, and it hits me that my last meal was a sugary bag of popcorn yesterday. I opt for a salad and some Doritos, and I sit far from my usual table to avoid the continued drama of my friends.

Armand finds me anyway. He makes a show out of slamming his tray down in front of him, dropping into a seat across from me, and leaning in until I'm forced to make eye contact.

"Uh, hi," I say.

"Dude, what the heck?" Armand is in full

big brother mode. I've heard him use this exact tone with his little sister.

I take a bite of my salad to avert his gaze. "Say what you're gonna say."

"You never texted me back last night." Armand doesn't back away. "I told you to text when you made it home, and I even texted you first. You never responded. After that whole thing with you and Seth last night, do you understand how that looks? I was forty percent sure you were dead in a ditch somewhere. I almost went to your house."

My gaze wanders to the other side of the cafeteria, where Miranda, Sun, and Seth have found their seats at our usual spot. Miranda catches my eyes for a second and gives me a quick wave.

"Well, thank you for *not* going to my house," I say. "I told my parents you drove me home, and then my mom threatened to take off my bedroom door for reasons and . . . yeah. For the record, I'd honestly rather be dead in a ditch than have you stir the pot." I put down my fork. "Wait. That's kind of a lot. You were *forty* percent sure I was dead, and you didn't come over? That's messed up."

"Don't spin this. Not funny and not the point." Armand finally leans back and starts on his spaghetti. "Because then you weren't even here before school this morning, and so by eight o'clock, I was *sixty* percent sure I'd accidentally killed you by letting you walk home. So, I texted you again. Radio silence."

"So, fun fact . . .. My phone is dead." I prove this by pulling out my phone and clicking the button a few times just to show him the black screen. "See? I fell asleep doing homework and forgot to put it on the charger."

"Uh-huh," Armand says. "Can we also talk about how you're wearing yesterday's clothes and you're barely focusing, and you look like the undead? Your hair's all . . .." Armand spreads his hands out over his head like I'm supposed to understand this.

I narrow my eyes and mirror his hands. "What does *this* even mean? Is that a moose?"

"And your eyes are all . . .." He looks at his hands, obviously struggling to come up with a bad gesture for whatever he wants to say. "Red, Isaac. They're all red."

"And?"

"It's just, the way all of this adds up is really

concerning." Armand weaves his fingertips together and stares me in the face. "Isaac, I'm gonna be upfront. I'm gonna ask you a serious question, and as your best friend, I expect a real answer. Whatever you say, I'll believe you, so please, don't take advantage of my trust. Okay?"

Oh gosh. I think I know what he's about to accuse me of, and it's humiliating. I cross my arms and sink down in my seat. "Fine."

"Are you playing *Galaxy's Oceans* online again? Without me?"

SEVEN

JACK

When I wake up on the third day, the conditions are even stranger than before.

This time, daylight streams into Isaac's room and he's nowhere to be found. Instead, *she*'s here.

The Winter Queen has found me.

Nev leans against the wall and looks out the window, still in all her wintery glory— fur and feathers, silver satin, and eyelashes, her white hair gathered into a cloud on top of her head. Her arms are crossed, and she drums her fingers against her elbows. It's the only sound in the room.

She turns to me, her gaze cold and unfeeling.

"Did you sleep well?"

Instinctively my hand goes to my belt, but then I remember I've lost my dagger. Frantically, I spring from the bed—the comfiest I've ever slept in, by the way—and look for a weapon. Something I can throw at her.

"Oh, relax." Nev rolls her eyes. "I'm not going to harm you. Not here. Not today."

I scoot back against the wall, my heart racing against my ribs. "What have you done to me? What is all this?"

"I told you," Nev says. "I'm giving you time to think. I don't suppose you've changed your mind about my daughter yet, have you? That would make things much easier for the both of us. I can't imagine you enjoy spending your daylight hours as a vegetable." Her violet eyes go to the bloody patch on my tunic. "When I designed this curse, I didn't expect you would get carried out of the labyrinth by some Earth dweller. I was rather angry until you got yourself stabbed. Then I thought, perhaps this is my finest curse. Earth dwellers love to destroy their pumpkins . . . and each other, for that matter. This has created a delightful experiment."

I make a pair of fists. Nev has no heart. I can't imagine how things are going back home since she cast me out. "I want to know that they're okay," I say. "Samuel. Aurora. My parents. My people."

Nev clucks her tongue. "Oh, you hurtful boy. They're all *my* people, too. I wouldn't dream of harming a hair on any of their precious heads, least of all my daughter. It's you who's wounded her by rejecting her love. What boy could possibly be so blind to her beauty and grace? You think there's something better waiting for you? Better than Aurora and a kingdom of snow?"

"I know your plans for Veron," I say. "I won't let you turn our world."

I see the muscles tighten in her jaw and for a second, Nev looks surprised.

Samuel's words come back to me. *You need to tread lightly.* This time, it's for his sake. I can't reveal that he's the reason I know about Nev's plot. If she finds out he's been spying on her since before the wedding, there's no way of knowing what she'll do to him.

"Whatever you think you know," Nev says slowly, "I highly advise that you adjust your narrative. I cursed you on behalf of love, darling. But I promise you the weather can change *very* quickly."

I narrow my eyes. "Yes, it can."

The Winter Queen sighs and paces the room, running a finger over various trinkets. "I'm tightening the parameters of my curse. Your attitude is far too vile. It will not serve my daughter or your people."

My heart quickens. She can't possibly make this worse.

"See, the original effects were set to transport you back to Veron at the end of seven days. Or when you solved the labyrinth, which was impossible, by the way. You were never getting out of there on your own. But seeing as how some Earth dweller carried you out, I have new conditions."

"You cheated," I say. "You made the labyrinth unsolvable?"

"No curse is truly unbreakable. I'm going to tell you exactly what you need to do. You insist that you cannot marry my Aurora, so I'm giving you until what the Earth dwellers call *Friday* to do better." She produces an old leather book out of thin air, slaps it on Isaac's desk, and turns to a random page in the middle. "Ah, yes. This ingredient is a little too common for my usual spell, but it is quite effective. You, my dear, have until Friday at midnight to acquire true love if you want your freedom. Then, and only then, will I reconsider the union between our houses."

My eyes nearly pop out of my skull. "True love?! In just a few days?" I'm no better off than I was on my wedding day, being asked to declare love for someone I'd just met. And who am I going to meet when I'm spending all my daylight hours as a vegetable? "It's not possible."

I don't even know what love is. It's always been arranged for me and for every royal I know. A puppet show. Here's this puppet. Here's that puppet. Now marry, produce an heir, and rule. The end.

Nev shrugs. "You can always opt out another way and say *I do*, which will bind you to Aurora until death do you part. That's much simpler, but seeing as how you like a challenge, who am I to deny you?" Gesturing out the window, she says, "Hmm. It's actually lovely here. I almost hope you win.

The Kingdom of Utono looked a lot like this when it existed. But I still prefer the winter."

She takes a sweeping step toward me and leans in, her breath cold against my neck. "Now, if you don't say *I do* or find true love by Friday at midnight, you will be cursed in your pumpkin form forever. At least, as long as pumpkins live. I expect you'll meet the Gray Lady and rot and feed the Earth within a few days' time. It's a good deed, really. And of course, you can't tell anyone the terms of the curse because that would be cheating."

I shake my head, dread filling my lungs. "This is cruel, Nev . . . even for you."

"You will address me as Your Majesty. Until Friday. By then, you may even be calling me *mother*!" Nev lets out a laugh and rises onto her tiptoes in apparent delight. "Oh, yes, this is my finest curse indeed. I sincerely look forward to watching the rest of this play out. Have you a bit of that curious Earth dweller food? Popcorn, I believe they call it?"

My jaws tighten. I can feel a headache coming on, a dull pressure inside my skull. "Are you done yet?"

Nev puts a finger to her chin. "Hmm, no. I

have one final gift. Call it an early wedding present. I will shorten your daily pumpkin hours just a smidge," she pinches two fingers together in front of her face, "to give you a fighting chance. You can have some of your daylight back, and perhaps, I'll even reserve your pumpkin form for sleep. I'm fascinated by the pursuit of true love. Do what you do, handsome. Go slay the dragon. Rescue the princess from the wicked queen. It's not so easy here. But you do have the gift of daylight, so I suggest you use it wisely."

"I'll treasure it forever," I drone.

"You are welcome, dearest." Nev gestures broadly at everything and says, "Good luck with all *this*. I'll see you Friday."

And just like that, the Winter Queen disappears, a thin silver vapor drifting out the window and melting into daylight.

Time becomes the wind. Stars and gods, I can feel every second of it, a grain of sand dripping from my fingers.

EIGHT

ISAAC

Armand seems fine after I promise him that I haven't been playing online RPGs without him. *Galaxy's Oceans* was a major keystone in the early days of our friendship, and it also had the unfortunate side effect of being so addictive, my grades slipped. My mom cut off that addiction right away.

"Just . . . if you were playing again, would you tell me?" Armand asks.

"Obviously," I say. "The galaxies wouldn't have been as fun without you. *Or* the oceans."

"You best remember," Armand says. "We're a team."

We bump knuckles to lock it in.

"So, are you sure there's nothing else

bothering you?" Armand asks. "Just the Seth thing? You just need more time with that?"

"Nothing else that I can explain right now," I say. "Just need time."

"I get it," Armand says. "But if you're still down for Fall Ball on Friday, I know Miranda still wants to go. It could be the three of us. Seth and Sun would be okay doing their own thing."

"I don't know if it's a good idea." Being in the same gym as Seth while people are slow-dancing and stuff is sure to kick up all kinds of feelings. "It's just too raw."

Armand nods. "That's cool. So, you wanna do something else? You can chill at my place, or we can catch a movie or whatever."

Probably for the first time all day, I smile. I don't deserve Armand. I'm sure people look at us sometimes and wonder if we're a "thing" because of the bond we share. It's the way people like to sort each other into neat little boxes. I did that when I first saw Armand in all his goth apparel and assumed he listened to death metal. Other people lose their minds when they find out I'm Hispanic because they don't find me Hispanic enough—as if there's only one way to be anything. And some people are surprised that Armand and I aren't in love, as if a gay dude is clearly into every guy he's friends with. We're never as simple as the boxes we stuff each other into, but one thing in my life has always been simple, even if it's only to the two of us.

I'm gay, Armand's straight, and he's the brother I've never had. That's it.

I finish my lunch and crush my milk carton. "I think you should go with Miranda to the Fall Ball," I say. "Or with everyone else. It could still be really fun. Plus, Miranda's been talking about her Silver Sorceress costume for days, so she needs to go show it off with someone."

"And let you bum around by yourself? What are you gonna do?"

"I'm gonna hand out candy, hang out with my parents, and look forward to your play-by-play of the night. All the costume fails. Teachers embarrassing themselves. Unfortunate dance moves. You can tell me all about how ridiculous it is, and then I'll get the full experience with none of the heartache."

"Well, I guess that's logical. And yeah,

Miranda would be furious if she didn't get to go rock her costume."

Something about this warms my heart. It feels normal. Friends talking about costumes around Halloween. At one point, we were all talking about a group theme and almost landed on the *Scooby-Doo* gang. Then Miranda went rogue, and it was every person for themselves.

"Do you already have a costume?" I ask.

Armand turns a little bit red and rubs the back of his neck. "I was thinking about Link from Zelda . . . make myself a Master Shield and wear a bunch of green. Thoughts?"

I have a hard time matching the tiny, blond, elfish Link with the tall, lanky Armand and his inky dark hair. But this is Halloween, a time to break all those boxes and be whoever the heck we want to be. "Link," I murmur. "Courageous and awesome. There's no one more fitting to save everyone—especially Princess Zelda—than Armand, the hero of Hyrule."

Armand lights up and goes back to his spaghetti. "All right, cool. Link, it is. Courageous and awesome. That was really nice, man."

"Aw shucks."

The doors of the cafeteria thunder open.

A boy runs in screaming at the top of his lungs. "I'm here to save you all!" His voice echoes and shuts down all other voices in the cafeteria. All eyes converge on him, and he stands in front of us drenched in sweat. "From the dragon! Where is the dragon? I'm here to slay him!"

The cafeteria goes dead quiet and time expands into infinity when I recognize the boy.

Tall and lean. Blue eyes. Reddish brown hair that falls in thick waves.

Or more obviously, he's dressed like he just ran away from a long day working the Renaissance fair.

The prince. Jack, he said his name was.

A burst of noise rolls through the cafeteria. I catch bits and pieces—mostly laughter and murmurings of "stupid" and "who's that?" I think the bell even rings to signal the end of lunch, but mostly, there's just blood rushing to my ears.

And then we lock eyes.

Jack runs for me and cuts through the crowd, swimming upstream as everyone else files out the doors. Some folks stop to take pictures of the stranger in the cafeteria—the boy who cried dragon—and they move on with their day. I'm frozen to the table until Jack gets to me.

"Isaac." Jack grabs my shoulder. "I saw the sign outside about the Belhaven dragon. Has he been defeated?"

Armand buries a hand in his hair, looking from me to the prince, and then from the prince back to me. "Uh, Isaac, who's this?"

The prince lets go of my shoulder and bows to Armand. "I am Prince Jack of the Kingdom of Veron. I'm here to slay the dragon. Is there a princess to rescue?"

Armand covers his mouth with a fist, barely suppressing a snicker. "Okay." He stands and pushes in his chair. "I'm not gonna ask anything more. I'll see ya, Isaac."

As Armand walks away, Jack looks around the cafeteria. It's basically just the two of us now.

Before I can stop myself, I'm on my feet and I'm digging my thumbs into Jack's shoulders.

"Who are you *really*?"

"Why, I'm Prince Jack of—"

"Cut that out," I snap. "It's not funny anymore. I know you don't go to this school. How did you make it past the guards without a school ID?"

Jack's eyes widen like he doesn't know what planet he's on. "Guards?" he says. "I didn't see guards. I climbed the fence and heard all the noise in here, and I thought this had to be where the Belhaven dragon was. I was trying to save everyone."

"That's the school mascot." I let go of Jack's shoulders, and he rubs them, wincing as though in pain. It's enough to make me feel bad, so I cram my hands into my pockets. "How did you do that pumpkin thing last night?"

Jack leans in, his voice broken. "I can't tell you everything, but . . . but, Sir Isaac, I've been cursed." I just about melt when I see his eyes shimmer with unshed tears. "It's all very strange and difficult to explain, but I'm all alone. And I'm somewhat afraid. Yet *you* rescued me from the corn labyrinth. I feel that maybe I can trust you."

Breakthrough—now I know other people can see Jack. He's not a hallucination.

Breakthrough—my strongest theory so far has been that this is all an elaborate prank, but nobody is this great of an actor. And even if there is, nobody I know can afford to hire them, or the theatrical pumpkin effects.

"I'm alone," Jack repeats, barely a whisper.

The case doesn't feel closed, but I've settled on one truth. This Jack guy needs help. I'm not sure what kind yet. Psychiatric? Social? Financial? I don't know. But I don't think he's harmful, and I think maybe I can be a starting point for him. If nothing else, I can listen and point him in another direction.

I take a deep breath and put a hand on the prince's back, guiding him toward the door with me. "Okay. Stick with me for a while, all right? I need to try to get out of my last two classes, and then we're going to get you some help."

Jack's face lights up like a Christmas tree. "Really? Oh, stars and gods. All my gratitude to you, Sir Isaac. You're too kind." He lowers his voice and looks around. "So . . . are you sure there is no dragon?"

"No." I can't help but look around and make sure the security guard's son isn't running around in the costume today. "And I have a rule. We need to stop at the nurse's office so I can get out of school. When we're there, you don't get to talk, okay? You let me do all the talking."

"I understand, Sir Isaac."

"And I have another rule. My name is *Isaac*, not *Sir Isaac*."

"I understand, Isaac."

"Good man."

We get some funny looks on the way to the nurse's office. People make their way to class, and here I am with this flashy royal who looks like his brain has been fried by playing too much *Galaxy's Oceans*. I even cross paths with Sun, who taps my arm and gives me a little smile before wrinkling her brows at Jack. I'm filled with relief that she doesn't hate me, then dread that she's about to ask about the prince.

"Hey. Classroom's the other way. Aren't you coming to history?" she asks. When she speaks the word *history*, her gaze cuts to Jack again, who looks like he's climbed out of the creases of our textbook.

A crew of big guys in letterman jackets walk by, snickering and pointing. "Halloween's Friday, bro!" one of them calls.

Jack scratches his head and stares after the jocks. "Hollow Wene . . .."

"I'm not coming to history today," I tell Sun. "It's a long story."

She looks at Jack again, and I can feel her preparing to introduce herself. I cut her off and ask, "Hey, are you and I okay?"

Sun blinks as if she's snapped out of a trance. "We still have some, um . . . talking to do, but we'll figure it out. We always do. Text me later?"

"You got it." I tap Jack again and cue him onward. "I gotta go. Have fun in history."

"Yay," she deadpans.

A million Fall Ball flyers and a pair of double doors later, we reach the nurse's office, the scent of bubblegum filling my nose. I put a finger to my lips as a reminder to Jack.

"Zoe," I whine. I only get to call her Zoe because she's my mom's friend and has known me all my life. "I'm not feeling so good today. Can I go home?"

Zoe gives me a worried look. "Aw, hi, *mijo*. I was hoping you were just coming to give me a hug and say hi!" Which I do sometimes. Yeah, I'm that nerd. "I'm sorry you're not feeling well. What hurts?"

"I threw up in bio." I hold my stomach, relieved that I don't have to lie.

Only now does Zoe seem to notice the ritzy stranger I've brought with me. She frowns and does a double take. "Who are you?"

Jack looks at me. "I'm not allowed to speak."

"Oh?" Zoe cuts her gaze to me, confused.

I bite my tongue and a hot breath comes out of my nose.

"Zoe, this is my, uh . . . cousin. Jack. His school is on fall break so he's visiting from out of town and came to pick me up. He just forgot to grab his visitor badge." So much for not having to lie.

Zoe chews on her lip, red and plump. "I didn't know you had a cousin." She thinks for a minute. "So, I guess I don't need to call your mom to come get you."

"No, you most certainly do not need to call my mom," I blurt. "Or my dad. No, ma'am. There'll be no need for that today."

Zoe looks at each of us in turn, as if she's trying to make a decision about something. "Okay, *mijo*. You're excused. Make sure you drink plenty of water and get some rest, okay?"

Win.

I give Zoe a weak, fake-sick smile. "Thank you." I take Jack by the arm and escort him to the door. "Let's go, cousin of mine."

"It's very nice to meet you, Isaac's cousin," Zoe says to Jack.

His jaws work like he wants to answer, but he traps the words inside, and it's almost like the silence pains him. This is my overall perception of the guy. He seems *trapped*. Wrapped in something bigger than my understanding. I wonder if I can help him untangle it.

"Tell me everything," I say on the way out.

"Stars and gods, where to begin?" Jack puts a hand to his forehead. "Well, I come from the Kingdom of Veron, and I've sort of been banished for the time being . . ."

And as threads of his story unfold, I wonder what else this Jack has trapped inside of him.

NINE

ISAAC

After four in the afternoon, my ears grow hypersensitive to the car pulling in the driveway. I've been in my bedroom listening for it, bracing myself, and re-running my plan ad nauseum for the past few hours. The car door slams. The keys jingle. The front door rumbles, and I take a deep breath for what's coming next.

"Isaac Jonathan Costa!"

Three names—one for every level of danger I'm in.

I shuffle down the stairs, dragging my feet until I find my mom in her scrubs. She slams her purse and keys onto the kitchen counter, puts her hands on her hips, and stares daggers at me. "Isaac. Why were you late to school this morning?"

Because of course she knows. These darn small towns. Everyone knows everyone. Mentally, I start booking a one-way ticket to a big, sprawling city like Vegas where I can live in the shadows.

I sink into the couch and play with a loose thread on one of the cushions. "I fell asleep doing my homework last night, and because of that, I forgot to charge my phone and set an alarm."

"*Ayy*," my mom says. "You went out to the farm with your friends and you didn't even have your homework done? That's never happening again. You're supposed to be on top of these things, and you know this. I cannot afford to pay for your college one day."

My heart sinks. This is the part of the talk that always shreds it into ribbons.

"Your papa and I have tried to work our way up in this life so we could make you a better future, but the system hasn't worked for us, *mijo*. You have to be the one to break the cycle, and the important work starts now. Colleges are going to ask for your freshman grades, and here you are, already slipping. From now on, you come straight home after school, and you do nothing until your homework is done. You do not go out, you do not send text messages, you do not play Nintendo, nothing. Home. Study. Then you can do whatever you want. I don't care what you do with the rest of your time, but your homework is non-negotiable." She draws out the last words and makes a chopping motion with her hand. "Do you understand?"

Every time she gives me this talk, it hurts when she talks about wishing she could give me more. Mom and Dad have already given me everything. I owe it to them to find my way to college one day. I just wish Mom understood that my present is important too, and it's taking up a heck of a lot more headspace than my future right now. "I understand, Ma."

"Good. Next time, I'll start waking you up at four-thirty."

Ouch.

"Tell me why you also left early," Mom says. "Are you really sick?"

Silently, I curse Zoe's name and her

friendship with my mom. Zoe's hug privileges are officially revoked.

"I threw up in bio," I say. "I wasn't feeling good, but I'm better now."

"Then who did you leave with?" Mom crosses her arms. "And don't say your *cousin*."

I release the zipper on the cushion. "It's really, really complicated."

"Complicated, huh? Is that code for you're not gonna tell me nothing?"

I sigh. "It just means it's complicated, Ma."

Mom is silent for a good minute. Then, just when I think she's about to let it go, she opens one of the drawers in the kitchen. She slips her hand in, and it comes out with a screwdriver. That's her "catch-all" drawer, with all the ketchup packets, instruction manuals she didn't want to throw away, and apparently, some basic tools. "Fine," she says. "You don't wanna talk to me? You don't get any more privacy. I warned you last night, so this is only fair."

Adrenaline floods my body when my mom begins the march up to my bedroom.

I spring up off the couch and follow her. "Okay, Mom." Everything else comes out in one breath. "Please understand something. Number one, I love you very much—"

Mom and I talk over each other the whole time.

"A bedroom door is a privilege, not a right—"

"—and I'm going to do my homework right now, actually—"

"—and it's like where did I even go wrong? You know—"

"—but you have to know that what you're about to see—"

"—was I like this with *my* mama? All these secrets and mood swings and—"

I squeeze past my mom and stand between her and my bedroom door, arms spread.

Mom looks like she's ready to detonate. Her voice is low, but oh . . . it's dangerous. "*Move.*"

I take a deep breath, hand on the doorknob. "Like I said, it's complicated, but just know that it can all be explained."

I open the door, and there on my bed sits Jack. Perfectly human. Zero percent pumpkin. We've been rehearsing this since I got home, and step one was to get him out of his royal duds and into something a bit more timely. He's in one of my old T-shirts—a concert tee from the first time I saw the Thunderlings—and a pair of basketball shorts. My shoes would obviously be too small, and my jeans are a bit too short, but the concert tee and the shorts are enough to make him look, well, *normal*. He twiddles his thumbs and doesn't look up until I speak.

"Mom," I say. "This is Jack. He's a new friend."

Jack stands and greets my mom, not with a bow like he originally wanted, but with a handshake like I taught him. The shake is a little awkward—Mom accepts hesitantly and when she connects with Jack, he goes up and down way too many times—but something about it has softened my mom's gaze. "I'm pleased to meet you," he says.

"Jack, this is my mom."

"Diana," my mom says.

"Now, Mom," I say, choosing my words carefully, "Jack doesn't go to my school. He's from just out of town. We met a really long time ago playing *Galaxy's Oceans* and kept in touch ever since. The thing is, he's recently been kicked out of his home. He doesn't have a place to stay right now." I pause and assess my mother's gaze, which is melting with every word. When she puts the screwdriver down on my dresser, I know it's time for the closer. "So, I offered to let him stay here for a while. *If* that's okay with you and Dad of course."

End speech. I hold my breath and wait for my mom to say something. Jack stares at his feet.

Technically, I'm not lying about Jack being kicked out of his home. At least, according to the story he told me. As he puts it, he's been cursed. He's from some distant place he calls Veron. He just wants to go home. I don't know how much to believe, but *he* believes it. The least I can do is listen and validate.

Before I know it, my mom has her arms out to Jack. "May I give you a hug, *mijo*?"

My soul rises up out of my body when he nods and they embrace.

I explained the term *mijo* more in depth to Jack earlier, out of fear that my mom would call him that and he would say something like, *But my name is Jack.*

"When you hear that," I had told him, "it's a term of endearment, like honey or sweetie or whatever. It means *my son*. And see, if my mom's okay with all this, she might call you *mijo*, too. It doesn't mean she really thinks you're her son, it just means she cares."

I don't know if he fully understood, but I think he does now. I knew my mom would come through. She doesn't ask why he was kicked out, and for that, I'm grateful.

I don't even know why the guy's been kicked out of his own kingdom.

"Any friend of Isaac is always welcome in my house," she says. "You can stay here as long as you like, Jack. Please."

The prince clasps my mom's hand in both of his and says, "Thank you."

My mom hugs me, too, and says, "I love you. What a nice friend you are. I'm going to start dinner soon if you and your friend are hungry. Just make sure you do your homework."

"Yes, of course!" I say. "Thank you, Ma."

And now I can exhale. I just tangled my own web a little bit, but for the first time, I feel okay about it. Like it'll all work out eventually. Mom will still need to tell Dad, but he'll be on board. There are other holes that I need to work out. Like what will I tell my parents if Jack spontaneously turns into a pumpkin in front of them? It may not be too hard to pretend I'm as shocked as they are. And I may have to be ready for a private talk with my parents tonight about how well I *really* know my "online friend," which is fair.

But for now, Mom smiles at Jack and leaves the room, closing the door behind her.

She doesn't even take her screwdriver.

TEN

JACK

Belhaven is so much stranger than Veron. Mr. Costa—Danny, as he prefers—is kind like his wife. He offers me some old clothes from his closet, a shaving kit, and some jokes that go over my head. Diana prepares a delicious meal of baked potatoes, steak, and salad. She and Danny seem eager to ask me questions, but Isaac insists that we eat in his room.

"You need to learn about some things first," Isaac says. "Plus, I don't want you turning into a pumpkin at dinner. Is that gonna happen again?"

"It happens when I sleep." I remember my earlier conversation with Nev. I wonder if I can really trust her to keep her word. "I think."

"Wild." Isaac looks confused but doesn't pry. Instead, he introduces me to the machine he calls his TV, which is oddly like a wizard's glass but the images are much crisper.

"Is this someone's future?" I ask him. "Is this *your* future?"

"No, you goof. This is a show." Isaac thinks for a moment. "You do have theater in your . . . kingdom or whatever, right? Entertainment?"

"Ah! Yes! Puppet shows!"

Isaac raises a brow. "Okay. Think of this as a puppet show, but with people. Entertainment."

It's the best puppet show I've ever seen, and it teaches me more about the world— how people dress, how they talk, what a smartphone is. The sorcery here is fascinating.

After the show, Isaac says, "Did you need to take a shower or anything? It's probably been a while, huh?" Seeing the blank look on my face, he rolls his eyes. "You don't even have showers, do you? Please tell me you have baths."

"Baths!" I snap my fingers. "Yes. I haven't

had a bath since my wedding day."

Isaac chokes on air and breaks into a coughing fit. "Hold up. You're *married*?"

I shake my head. "No. It's a long story." There's only so much I can tell him. I keep thinking of the Winter Queen's conditions. If I reveal too much, I'll lose and become a pumpkin forever. "But I'm not married."

"Whew," Isaac says. "I don't know if I can house two people."

"What's a shower?" I ask, eager to change the subject.

Isaac grins and rubs his hands together. "Get ready for the most luxurious bathing experience of your life."

He guides me to their washroom and shows me a series of dials and knobs in the wall. Hot. Cold. Pressure. I play with the knobs until I find a comfortable temperature. Then Isaac hands me a bar of green soap. "When you're ready, you turn the middle one, and it all comes down like rain. Oh, and pro tip, turn the knob first, *then* get in and shut the curtain behind you."

I look at the water in fascination. This is a lot of information.

"I'm in the next room if you have questions. Just, you know, do me a favor and please put clothes back on when you're done?"

My jaw drops. "But of course!"

"Just making sure." Isaac laughs and closes the door. "Have fun."

He wasn't lying. The shower is the most luxurious bathing experience of my life. The water comes down on my back and pounds my worries away like a massage. Nev. Curses. Loneliness. I never want the shower to end.

When I get out, Diana comes up to Isaac's room.

"Jack, *mijo*," she says. "I made you a bed downstairs. Our couch pulls out and there's pillows and blankets and TV. There's this weird broken spring in the couch, but it's still pretty comfortable. I hope you'll sleep well on it."

"Um . . . actually, Ma," Isaac says. "Jack's gonna sleep in here if that's okay."

Diana wrinkles her brows. "On the floor?"

"I'll make sure he's comfy," Isaac says. "It's just that after all he's been through, it can be good to have someone around. Plus, honestly, the couch isn't that comfy. I always feel the spring."

Diana sighs. "Jack, is that really okay with you? I don't want you to sleep on the floor."

"It's fine," I say. "The floor can be nice. I can sleep well on bales of hay."

The corners of her lips quirk up.

"Or I'll even sleep on the floor," Isaac says. "Jack can have my bed."

Diana gives her son a soft look, and says, "Okay. I'll bring up the pillows and blankets. Door open, though."

Isaac chews his lip. I know he's doing everything he can to make sure nobody else sees my cursed form. "Half-open?"

"Half-open."

With Diana's pillows and blankets, Isaac builds a little cot on the floor, and I lie down before he can claim it. After all, I won't need the comfort of a real bed once I drift off. I'd even be fine on the dresser.

"We'll swap each night, deal?" Isaac says. "And listen, I need to go to school tomorrow. My parents will be at work. Will you be okay on your own?"

Tomorrow. One day closer to Friday. Being alone may be the perfect opportunity to go and look for true love. "I'll be fine."

"You can either stay here or, I guess go wander, but if you go out, be back before three and *please,* don't be weird. You're my responsibility right now, so don't go looking for dragons or danger or anything. And don't come to my school again. Go to the library or the mall or something. I'll give you some of my allowance."

"*Maul*?" Lion pits and gladiator arenas?

"Mall. Shopping? Food? Lots of people everywhere? Man, you have a lot to learn." He closes the door halfway, jumps into bed, and flicks off the lights. "But we'll get there. Good night, Jack."

"Good night, Isaac."

I stare at the ceiling, processing the day until my eyes grow heavy.

TUESDAY, OCTOBER 28

THE CURSE OF MELODIES

ELEVEN

ISAAC

It's Tuesday morning, and I'm not late for school. In fact, I'm about twenty minutes early, and this is my usual time to have breakfast with my friends. Miranda joins me and Armand today. The first thing she does is lightly bounce her hand on top of my head a few times.

"Your hair's so nice," she says. "I missed it."

I touch my hair to make sure she didn't mess it up too badly, blushing a little. "Thanks, Rand."

"How are you?" Miranda says. "I've been thinking of you. Armand says you're not coming to the Fall Ball anymore, and I hope you know I'm still coming over to show off my costume. You have no choice."

She's so flat and serious when she says this, and it makes me spit up some of my chocolate milk when I can't stop the laughter. "I expect no less. Can't wait to see you rock it."

Armand jumps right into the action. "Okay, enough small talk. Isaac. Inquiring minds want to know: What was the deal with that dude in the cafeteria yesterday?"

Miranda leans in, resting on her elbows. "Ooh, yes. I'm curious about that, too. He was all over WowFeed after lunch. Some people even edited a dragon into the picture. Me, I just thought he was super cute. But anyway."

Somehow, I doubt they'll buy the same story I told my parents—the whole *Galaxy's Oceans* thing. Mom and Dad bought it because they understand nothing about *Galaxy's Oceans*. But if I tell Miranda and Armanda that Jack's a friend from out of town, they'll see right through me.

This little group we've built? They're kind of my only friends. I mean, it's not like I don't like anybody else or that I'm perceived as a loser or anything, at least by *most* people. Coming out did reveal a few bad apples at school who suddenly felt they were too cool to breathe the same air as me. But for the most part, when people find out I'm gay, it's no more significant than me saying I like pizza. I just don't have a lot of people that I'd naturally bring home from school or share lunch with. That's all.

I decide to start with half-truths and test the waters.

"Well," I say, "his name's Jack. He doesn't go here."

Armand and Miranda say nothing. Their faces are all like, *go on.*

"He lost his home and doesn't really have a place to stay."

Miranda frowns. "Ooh, that must be rough."

"My family's taking him in for a while until he can get back on his feet."

Armand grins. "That's so cool of your family. How come you barely mentioned him? We spent all day with you on Sunday, this guy comes to school on Monday like he already knows you, and now you tell us he's living with you? Didn't I last go to your house like, Friday night?"

"It's a sensitive thing," I say. "I feel bad for the guy. It doesn't feel right telling his whole story. There's probably some trauma there, and if it were me, I wouldn't want the world sharing. He's not looking for pity or handouts or anything. Just a place to stay, and I'm trying to be a friend."

"Now I get why you've been acting so weird!" Armand slaps a palm on the table for emphasis. "That's a big change, taking someone into your house like that. Where is he even from? I mean, how do you know him?"

I stare into my chocolate milk. "*Galaxy's Oceans.*"

"I knew you were playing without me again! What the heck, man?"

"No, from a long time ago. We just kept in touch, like on WowFeed and stuff."

"I didn't know you made a real-life friend on *Galaxy's*. What was his avatar's name?"

Sweat beads up on my forehead. "Uh, JackOLantern123, I think. I could be wrong. He retired his character."

Armand thinks for a minute. "I think I remember a JackOLantern guy. He was a Space Elf? Classed as a Moon Mage and specializing in Lunar Alchemy?"

"That's the one," I drone.

Miranda yawns. "You two are such nerds. Do you even listen to yourselves?"

"Said the Silver Sorceress," Armand says.

"No, see, look." Miranda puts both hands in front of her face, palms parallel to the ground. "This is the nerd meter. I'm right here because of my love for comics, math, and a good book." She wiggles one hand in front of her face. "I'm comfortable here. Now for you two." She stands on her toes and stretches the other arm way over her head. "Ugh, you just broke my scale. You're the worst."

Armand and I share a crisp high five.

Miranda flops back down and sits on her knees. "But I think it's really sweet what you're doing for your friend." She takes a sip of water and adds, "I know you're letting him adjust and everything, but do you think we'll get to meet him soon?"

I almost cringe at the awkward possibilities. Jack did well with my parents last night, but not from a lack of coaching and an insistence that he let me do at least eighty percent of the talking. I imagine him mingling with my social group and how much side-eye he would get for all his "stars and gods" and childlike wonder at the simplest of things. It was a miracle he figured out how to turn off the shower last night. I wonder how he'd react in a computer store or inside a car.

"We'll take things one day at a time," I say. "When he seems ready, I'll introduce you."

"That's fair." Miranda flushes and averts my gaze. "*Maybe* you can even set up a date? Nudge-nudge? Wink-wink?"

I almost spit up chocolate milk again. Wait until Miranda learns Jack's married, or not married, or whatever the real story is. I have so much to learn about him. I'm not even a hundred percent sure that Jack's a cursed prince from Veron or wherever he says he's from. Maybe ninety percent on account of the weird pumpkin thing—nothing seems "cursier" than turning into a pumpkin at night—but what if Jack's just a phenomenal illusionist who bumped his head a little too hard performing a magic trick one day? So hard that it knocked his mind all the way back to like, the Renaissance? How would I ever disprove that?

Armand saves me by shaking his head. "You and Isaac's friend? I don't see it, Miranda."

Miranda takes a deep breath and exhales a dreamy sigh. I can practically see the little heart bubbles popping above her head. "A girl can dream. It's cool. At least there's always the Hemsworths. Or Diego Rosas. He's still single, right?"

I scratch my head. "The *Off the Beaten Path* guy?" My gaze trails to a poster on the cafeteria wall, where a handsome TV star tells us to *Eat right, exercise, and climb your mountain!* "Good luck with that. You might have a better chance with his nephew Charlie, though. He and his twin sister started a vlog recently, and I think they're about our age."

"There's a Charlie Rosas? Hmm, must learn more." Stroking her chin, Miranda pulls out her phone and runs a search.

Armand puts his hands to his face, palms horizontal. "Miranda, this is the fangirl meter. Isaac and I are right here—"

Miranda shoves her hand in Armand's face. "This is the door. Woman at work."

When the bell rings to head to class, my spirits are high and my heart is full. This doesn't feel like the kind of day where I'll get sick in biology and have to apologize to Mrs. McKelvey.

But my mind still wanders. How is Jack spending his day alone? I flash back to yesterday at lunch and I keep thinking, *Please, Jack. Please don't get yourself into trouble.*

TWELVE

JACK

Tuesday feels magical and dances with promise.

I remembered how to take a shower.

I've fit myself into one of Isaac's shirts and a pair of Danny's pants he called *jeans*, which are nearly a perfect fit.

With the shaving kit, I polish up. The crystal bottle labeled *aftershave* is something new to me, and I almost think it's a potion meant for drinking until I see the warning label on the back. I pump a little spray onto my wrist, waft in the scent, and am pleasantly surprised by its musk. So, I spray it all over. I run a comb through my hair, and I study my look in the mirror. I don't feel natural, but I suppose this is the look in Belhaven.

And a good look is exactly what I need, because today I'm looking for my true love.

Isaac said something last night that sinks into my brain—the *maul* is a place where there are a lot of people. And if one is looking for love, perhaps one would go to a place where there are a lot of people.

I leave the house and get on one of those giant magic vessels called buses, because on TV the bus seems to take people wherever they wanted to go. As soon as I get on, the driver pinches her nose and waves her hand in front of her like I smell bad or something, which is rude because I took a shower and used aftershave.

"I'd like to go to the *maul*," I say.

"Okay, okay." The driver shuts the door and seems eager to take off. "Have a seat. Fashion Square's five stops away. And it's Free Ride Tuesday, so don't worry about fare."

The Fashion Square is a cute outdoor plaza that reminds me of one of the gathering spaces back home. A marble fountain stands high in the center. Like all the light posts, it's decorated with pumpkins and ghosts. People throw coins into the water, and some take photographs on their smartphones, which I still find fascinating. Back home, an artist had to paint you in a special moment, and it would take hours or sometimes days.

Delicious scents fill the air, and I don't recognize most of them. But the most complex, divine, and pungent smell attacks me like a love potion, and I trace it to a pretty young woman sitting on a bench under one of the light posts. When I see her, I grow dizzy. She looks something like Aurora, but her hair is red and her ears aren't pointed like the Inverans'.

She gives me a smile from afar. I rub the back of my neck and work up the courage to approach her.

"Hello, fair lady," I say.

My heart sinks when she gives me the same disgusted look as the bus driver. She covers her nose and stands, coughing into her jacket. "Oh, that smell! It's so strong!"

"Wait!" I say before she can walk away. I take a deep breath, inhaling that divine scent. I point to her paper plate. "That food triangle you're holding . . .. I must know what it is as if my life depends on it."

The young lady shakes her head at me and scoffs. "It's pizza, duh. What planet are you from?"

"I'm from Veron," I say.

"Well, when you go back to . . . wherever, teach them not to use so much aftershave!" She runs away gagging, carrying the mystic nourishment known as pizza away with her.

Many people walk around Fashion Square with triangles of pizza, and I don't need much time to trace them back to a vendor stand with a red, white, and green-striped flag that says *Petrelli's* on it. I race to the vendor and say, "How much gold for the pizza?"

The mustached man turns red from laughing so hard, and I don't understand what's funny. "Ho, boy!" He whistles and slaps his thigh. "Let's start from the beginning. You want cheese, pepperoni, or veggie?"

My gaze goes to an entire circle of the beautiful substance, a full sunburst resting on the counter. Steam dances off the cheesy surface in hypnotic swirls, vanishing into nothing. I point to the circle. "That one. I want all of that one."

The man laughs even harder. "Nice! Someone's got a big appetite. It's gonna be a few minutes for a whole pepperoni pizza, but sure, I'll make it for ya."

I resist the urge to hug the man. "Much gratitude to you, sir!"

"Yeah, sure. It's the job." He punches some buttons on his machine, and green numbers light up on a screen. "Fifteen dollars, my friend."

I pull out the wad of currency Isaac left me. It's all foreign to me, so I empty the full wad onto the counter and let the man take it.

He scoops up the small pile I've made, and now he's laughing so hard, I'm concerned that he's under a curse of his own. Samuel and I thought of this before—a curse of uncontrollable, maddening giggles that plague you until your sides burst. I'm still not sure how I'd fight that one, except to maybe think of something hopelessly sad.

"This is forty dollars," the man says. "Who *are* you?"

"I'm Pr— I'm Jack," I say simply, remembering Isaac's coaching. "Just Jack."

"Well, Just Jack." The man counts out some

new currency and hands me a stack of it. "Wait about ten minutes and I'll have a fresh pepperoni pizza ready for you."

"Lovely," I say.

Yesterday I could feel minutes dripping between my fingers like water. Waiting ten minutes for the pizza feels like my own private eternity. My stomach groans. Weeps. I must see a million strangers walking around with their own triangles of pizza and other tasty-looking foods I've never seen before.

I'm intrigued by the beverages people walk around with, bottles of fizzy brown substance that fall out of a large money machine. While I wait for my pizza, I pay the money machine and select a bottle. When I take the first sip, the cold, sweet bubbles burst against my tongue and it's the oddest sensation, like stars in a bottle. And I never want it to end.

At long last, the man at *Petrelli's* hands me my pizza in a large, thin box. I feel as though I've received the best gift in the world.

"Have fun!" he tells me.

I take my gift to an empty table, open the box, and peel a greasy triangle away from the circle. With the first bite, warm cheese, sweet tomato, thick crust, and salty meat fill my life with meaning.

I have discovered true love.

After two slices, my stomach is full, so I stop eating and carry the box with me as I explore the shops of Fashion Square. Many of the merchants look at me like they want to take the box away, and I understand why they covet my pizza. Luckily they leave me and my true love alone.

I enjoy looking around the stores, but the forty dollars I've been left with doesn't cover much more than the pizza. In a clothing shop, I try on a handsome leather jacket that fits me perfectly, and the worker asks for "one-sixty-five seventy." The wad of currency comes out of my pocket again and I push the whole thing toward him. This worker isn't as nice as the *Petrelli's* man, because he shoves it all back to me, takes the jacket away, and demands that I leave his store.

In another shop, I find walls and walls of books, and my spirit sings. Reading has always been a joyful escape for me. Compared to Veron, Belhaven has an infinite selection. I collect a large stack, find a seat in the store, and flip through all of them until I find the perfect story: *The Once and Future King*. Camelot is a refreshing slice of home, without the awful threat of the Winter Queen or forced marriages. It's funny because I don't necessarily long for home, but reading the book fills a hole where I've lost familiarity over the past few days.

To my surprise, in spite of the hole filling up, there's also *heartbreak*. A pain in my chest that the story couldn't fill. I only wish it could tell me that Samuel, Aurora, and my parents are okay. This is all I want. I want their wellness and freedom and sunlight, even if I never have another lesson from Samuel or another banquet again.

It's almost enough to make me want to say the words that will set me free.

I do.

That's all it will take. Nev was right—it really would be simpler.

I close my eyes, open my mouth, and take a deep breath.

And my ears are filled with one of the most beautiful sounds I've ever heard.

Outside beyond the shop doors, music

plays. A lush melody fills the air, and its strings and winds express all the feelings that words cannot fill. The rise and fall of the refrain traces something in my heart that I can't speak. It's joyful and celebratory, yet it has mournful, melancholy undertones. It sings several emotions and experiences all at once, yet it doesn't speak a word.

I rise from my chair, leaving the books behind, taking only my pizza box.

Entranced, I follow the melody to the shop next door. *Bella's Music Emporium.*

A trio plays an assortment of instruments, and I recognize them all because I've play a few myself. A piano. A flute. A violin.

A guitar sits on a stand, untouched and begging to sing.

Without saying a word, I take a seat and pick up the instrument, and I join the melody. The original players look somewhat surprised, but they keep right on playing and welcome me into their shared vision. That vision takes hold of me like wind in my hair, and I lose myself in the music until time exists no more.

THIRTEEN

ISAAC

I find Jack at Fashion Square around five o'clock.

I've cycled through all kinds of emotions over the past few hours. When school ended and I came home to an empty room, I freaked. There was fear. There was anger. There was worry. And then there was anger again. I had told Jack to be home by three if he went out, so what was I supposed to think when he wasn't home? That he'd been kidnapped? That he'd wandered off and become a pumpkin in the middle of the street? That he was looking for dragons again?

First, I checked the library—the first place I told him to explore. I asked the librarians if they'd seen a guy a little taller than me, kind of strange, with dark hair and blue eyes. They explained that "this doesn't give us much to work with, but it's been pretty empty here today."

I checked the park, even going so far as to scour the playground and see if Jack got stuck in the slide or something. By the time I was done, I knew my mom would be getting home soon, and I couldn't put up with another one of her lectures. I raced back to beat her home and decided I'd let her know what was going on. Running through the neighborhood, I saw a *lot* of pumpkin guts on the sidewalks, and every single time, my stomach did a horrible twist.

When Mom came home, I waited for her at the front door. "Ma," I said, "I can't find Jack. I just wanted to let you know I'm going to Fashion Square to look for him. I think that's where he's at."

"Is your homework done?"

"No, but—"

Mom jingled her keys. "Get in the car and I'll drive you. You'll waste homework time taking the bus there and back. And I know you won't do your homework on the bus."

On the drive, we had a long talk, and she asked all the questions I knew were coming. No, I didn't know how long he'd be with us. No, I hadn't known him very long, but yes, I trusted him. No, he had no weapons in the house.

"If he's going to be with us for a long time," Mom said, "then he needs to enroll at Belhaven and go to school, okay? That's my main rule, and I'll tell him that myself. School and safety. That's all I care about."

On one hand, that sounded like a nightmare. Jack was already the laughingstock at Belhaven, and he wasn't even a student there. On the other hand, having him close by would be an excellent way to keep an eye out and make sure he didn't get himself into trouble.

Which brings me to Fashion Square, where Jack sits in *Bella's Music Emporium* surrounded by swooning and adoring strangers, a shiny new guitar in his hands. I'm surprised by how natural he looks with a guitar, like it's an extension of himself. And I'm even more surprised by the sound that he and the guitar produce together, rich and full and joyful, like the words he puts to his refrain:

"I've found a home away from home,
A place my soul just loves to roam,
Tell everybody not to wait up late for me,
'Cause I just got too much to do, too much to see,
Here in my home away from home."

As Jack plays, he's a new person. He's all raw emotion and confidence. It's like nothing exists but the song and the story he's created. He sways and leans into his melody, eyes closed and fingers dancing.

A couple of people record him on their phones, whispering to each other in admiration. The whole time, Jack takes no notice.

Until he looks up at me, and he stops mid-song. "Isaac!"

Applause bursts through the emporium, and Jack's little crowd rushes up to him.

"Oh my god, I just fell in love with you," a girl about my age says. "Can I have your number or your WowFeed?"

Jack blushes. "Love? Like true love?"

"Why sure, cutie." The girl giggles. "So . . . no number?"

People ask him for lessons, if he wants to

work in the emporium, if he wants to play at the local coffee shop, and if he wants to start a band. As he stumbles over the barrage of questions, I rush in and pat him on the back. "Hey, buddy, that was great!" I say. "We need to get home. My mom's waiting in the car."

Jack sets down the guitar, bows, and grabs a pizza box under his chair. And we're out.

Crossing the outdoor mall and heading to the car, I first hit him with the lecture. "I told you to be home by three, man. What were you doing? You had me all scared."

"I'm sorry. I started playing and I lost time. I couldn't stop. It was like magic." Jack talks faster than usual, the words coming out in an excited rush and he waves his pizza box all over. "I'm sorry I scared you."

I chuckle. It's hard to stay mad at him when I found him so happy. Seeing him all lit up and animated? It's nice. He doesn't seem so trapped right now.

"We're gonna find a way to keep in touch, okay?" I say. "Do you know how many smashed pumpkins I found in the streets looking for you today? It freaked me out a little."

"I'm sorry." Jack looks down. He's still wearing his dusty boots over his jeans. They stick out like neon lights in the dark, but other than that, he's dressed . . . well, *normally*.

"Stop saying you're sorry."

"I'm regretful."

I clap him on the shoulder and pull him in in a sort of buddy hug as we walk. "You don't have to be regretful. We'll figure out something for tomorrow. Just so I know you're okay."

"Okay." Jack seems happy about this. He shakes the box in his hands. "Isaac, have you ever had *pizza* before? Stars and gods, it's my favorite!"

I smirk. The thing is, people tolerate *Petrelli's* because it's everywhere, but it's also just *meh*. Actually, it's probably the worst pizza in town. But I don't tell Jack that. If it's his first pizza and he loved it, I'm gonna let him enjoy it.

"You have so many amazing experiences ahead, my friend," I say. "Pizza's just the tip of the iceberg."

When we get in the car, my mom greets Jack with a hearty hello.

"Did you know Jack's a music star?" I ask right away. "He just had a whole crowd in the music shop right now."

Mom grins in the rearview mirror. "Really, Jack? What do you play?"

"A lot of things," Jack says. "But today I found a guitar."

"It was insane," I say. "Jack, did you write that song yourself?"

"Yes," Jack says. "But I didn't write it. It just sort of fell out of my head while I played."

Mom drums on the steering wheel. "Danny plays the guitar, too! That's how I fell in love with him. Did I ever tell you that, Isaac?"

I rest my head against the window. "Only about forty bazillion times."

"So there I was, interviewing for my job at the hospital," she begins anyway. "And I was so nervous. I hadn't had my *cafecito* yet, my hair was all crazy, I had just broken up with my boyfriend, so my makeup was all gross. Then, five minutes before they call my name, the most beautiful man walks into the lobby holding a guitar. And everyone is all grumpy because they're sick or they're waiting for news or wanting to talk about their bills.

The beautiful man sits in the corner with his guitar and just starts playing without a care. And I'm thinking, *Who in the world is this fool?* Who is he to barge in and start making noise in the lobby? But oh, how everyone loved it. For a few minutes, they forgot about their worries, and I forgot about my crazy hair, and we all just got lost in his story. He took our pain away and brought us love and life."

Jack grins from ear to ear. "Did you go talk to him?"

"No," Mom says. "We locked eyes for a minute, and then they called my name to interview. I didn't see him again until later that day when I walked into the bakery to buy some comfort food. That's where he was working. He didn't have his guitar of course, but he remembered me from the lobby and gave me a free pastry. I thanked him for his song, and he asked about my interview. We didn't actually start dating until sometime later. But that's where the story began, and the rest is history."

Jack tilts his head back and smiles. "My mentor once taught me that music is a universal language. That its power can bring worlds together. And it brought your family together."

Mom nods in the mirror. "Yes, it did, *mijo*. Music brought me love, and love brought me Danny and Isaac. Come to think of it, I wonder where Danny stashed that old guitar."

Knowing my dad, it's probably gathering dust in a closet. He hasn't played in ages.

After a minute, Mom turns up the radio to share her own taste in music. She's all about that eighties rock, and apparently Jack likes it, too, because he taps his feet and keeps time on his pizza box.

"I thought I smelled pizza," Mom says. "Does that mean I don't need to cook tonight?"

"Isaac and I will finish this," Jack says.

"Woohoo," Mom says. "I'm wiped out, boys. Dad and I are gonna enjoy some leftovers and watch Housewives. And I thought maybe tomorrow we'd all go out for ice cream and a movie. As long as homework gets done, of course." She gives me a pointed look in the mirror. "Does that sound nice?"

I'm not sure Jack understands ice cream yet, so I jump in. "That could be fun."

"Lovely," Jack says.

Before we get back home, my phone lights up, and I'm happy to hear from Sun.

Hanging in there? Miss u.

I type back, **Hanging in there. How are you?**

**OK. Lots of homework = blah.
U still coming to the Fall Ball?**

**Idk. I don't think so.
Lots going on right now.**

I might break up with Seth. :(

Omg why? I hope it's not because of me. I know I kind of blew up on Sunday and I made things stupid and awkward. I regret it. I miss him, but I love you more. You deserve to be happy. And no, I'm not just saying that.

> I just want things to go back to normal. It feels like everything's changing.

> Tell me about it. :/

> :)

> Don't break up with Seth. Change can be a good thing. That's why we have seasons!

> True. Miranda told me about the friend that's staying with u. If I can be of any help, I just want u to remember that I'm here. I can help look for resources and stuff and if he needs anything. Or if u do, too.

> Thank you, friend. Hugs.

> Hugs to u.

Strangely, thinking of Seth doesn't twist my

heart into its usual knots. Instead, there's a sort of numbness there. Healing, I suppose.

But I understand that I can't avoid my friends forever, and I can't keep Jack a secret when he's making these waves in my world. Sunday, my home. Yesterday, my school. Today, the Fashion Square Mall. What's coming for tomorrow?

When we get home, I sit him down and we share pizza as we try to fill in the gaps in our knowledge.

"So, you're cursed," I say. "And this curse kicked you into my world, where sometimes you become a pumpkin."

"Yes."

"And you were . . . supposed to be married?" I phrase this delicately and decide to leave it here, because yesterday this didn't seem like something Jack wanted to go into detail about.

Jack takes a sip of his soda. Every time, his eyes go wide like it's a big surprise, but I can tell he loves it. "Yes," he says. And to my surprise, he tells me a little more. "I was engaged to be married to Princess Aurora Frost of the Winter Kingdom. Only the ceremony wasn't complete."

"I see." Mentally, I fill in the gaps.

The princess ran away from him at the altar.

My heart breaks for the guy, and I also wonder how it happened. If I'm honest and I look past the awkward mishaps of the past few days, Jack's kind of a catch. Good-looking. Good heart. Sweet. Not to mention, he's a musician. Who runs away from someone like Jack? I can't wrap my head around it.

Once again, I see the trapped boy and all the secrets boarded up inside of him. It's a look that makes me sad, but I figure these are all things that take time, like thawing a block of ice. We're not in any sort of hurry to break the walls.

"I'm sorry it didn't work out," I say. "It must be tough."

Jack gives me a little half-smile. "Thanks."

I slide the last slice of pizza over to him, and then I grab my laptop.

"So, this is how we'll keep in touch tomorrow. I have my smartphone, and you can take the laptop and use it to let me know if you're going anywhere. There's all these other things you can do, too!" I bring up a site in my browser. "I made you a playlist of all kinds of videos that'll teach you about life around here. How to understand money, social skills, pop culture, food . . . all the things."

Jack takes the laptop and runs a finger over the screen. "Stars and gods. It's like magic."

"Kinda," I say. "Just make sure you don't let the battery die. And then maybe sometime you can teach me more about your home."

Jack chuckles and runs a hand through his hair. "I feel there's not much to teach."

I wrinkle my brows. "Well, what makes you happy about it? When you think of home, what is it?"

Jack finishes off his pizza, thinking as he chews. His gaze rests on a spot on my wall. "It's friendship and duty . . . but it's also expectations. It's eternal summer."

"I never loved summer," I say. "Summer is humid here in Belhaven."

"I enjoy it," Jack says, "but it's missing something."

"What's it like being a prince? It must be nice being able to do whatever you want."

Jack sighs. "I do what I'm told. I be who

I'm told to be. Every day I'm training to be a better, stronger man. I wonder if I missed out on being a boy."

I want to ask him what the difference is and why he should have to choose, but I already know the answer. All our lives, boys are told to man up. No emotion. No weakness. Look this way, walk this way, talk this way. I can't imagine what kind of masculine pressure a *prince* must face.

Jack points to the spot on my wall. "Who's that?" he asks.

I laugh and unpin the poster he's been staring at. "This, my friend, is Chris D'Agosto. He's a musician like you. He's always been my favorite."

The ideal man in my eyes. Not because he looks, acts, or talks a certain way, but because he's confident in how he presents himself every time, whether he's sporting jeans and a five o'clock shadow or sequins and stage makeup.

Jack looks lost in thought as he stares at the poster. "Huh."

As if on cue, my mom and dad enter the room, and Dad cradles his prized guitar—

the same one that won him a woman and a future son.

Dad takes a long hard look at Jack. "I hear you're a star, *mijito*."

My jaw drops when Dad holds his guitar—basically his heart—out to Jack. I've never been allowed to touch the thing.

"Can you play me something?" Dad asks.

Jack blinks a few times, almost star struck by the old instrument.

"Go on," Dad says. "It won't bite you. Just want to hear a tune."

A few minutes later, we move into the living room where Jack plays for us for the rest of the night. When Jack touches a guitar, it amplifies him and suddenly, the rock star is back.

Mom rests her head on Dad's shoulder, their fingers intertwined. And I sprawl out on the carpet and soak up every note. Music really is a universal language, because for an hour or so, I feel like I'm a part of the world Jack comes from. I'm warmed by visions of summer and stung by notes of heartache and enthralled by a world of magic that can't be explained. Whether it exists or not, I don't care anymore. I'm just thrilled to share it for a little while.

When Jack finishes and hands the guitar back out to my dad, my jaw drops when Dad shakes his head.

The skin around Jack's eyes crinkles. "Sir?"

"It's *Danny*," Dad says. "And you have a real gift, *mijo*. You have something special in you. Something nobody can take away, and it shouldn't be wasted. I've played my last note. My passion is in baking now. If I keep this, I'm wasting its magic."

Jack looks down and runs a finger along the neck of the guitar. "I don't understand. This is a part of your story. It's your history."

"Yes. My story." Dad fixes his gaze on the old strings, a bittersweet half-smile on his face. He takes my mom's hand and they exchange a look of love, eyes soft and gleaming. "And I already got the ending I wanted. But the story of the guitar won't continue if I keep it. It'll just continue to gather dust, and that's not what it's made to do."

"Dad," I breathe. "What are you saying?"

Dad doesn't miss a beat before he says, "I'm saying it belongs to Jack now."

WEDNESDAY, OCTOBER 29

THE CURSE OF ICE CREAM AND LONELINESS

FOURTEEN

JACK

I spend Wednesday morning soaking up the magic of the internet.

Isaac's playlist teaches me a lot about his world. By the end of the first video, I think I understand Belhaven currency—dollars, quarters, pennies, and what have you. I still prefer gold, but my favorite is the tool they call a credit card. I don't understand how all the money gets inside of it, but magic is strange.

Another video teaches me how people talk around here, and it's like a whole different language. Nobody says *stars and gods* when they're excited; they say *wicked* or *sick*. Huh. Wicked, I guess.

I learn something about laundry, something

about clothes, and something about government. Democracy is fascinating. The people choose their kings and queens, or . . . *presidents*? I wonder if it's working. I wonder if Veron should try it.

The end of Isaac's playlist is a surprise—it's all music. I learn about The Charmers and The Lost Boys and Phil Vs. the Specters, but I'm most fascinated by The Vegas Thunderlings. Their songs are like medicine for a pain I didn't know I felt. By the end of the first song, I feel lighter. Happier. Like their words are straight out of a spell book. I'm mesmerized by their stage performance, not to mention Chris D'Agosto and all his charisma. I can see why he's Isaac's favorite.

When all the music ends, I click out of the playlist and another window appears. Isaac called this WowFeed. A photograph displays Isaac with a dark woman in silks and bangles and a blue pumpkin in their hands.

I've never seen myself sleeping, least of all during this bloody curse, but I know in my heart that the blue pumpkin is me.

The photograph belongs to a woman named Farmer Elaine, and the caption below reads:

One of my beloved visitors found this wicked gorgeous pumpkin in our haunted corn maze today! Just another magical day at the farm. What tricks and treats will you find at Farmer Elaine's? Come see me today!

I find a spray of comments under her caption:

Obviously fake.

How is it blue?!

My friends and I are going tonight! Want!

Will you still have pumpkin popcorn?

I bury my hands in my hair, dizzy with understanding. This Farmer Elaine is connected to my fate. In fact, I remember the undead monstrosity in the corn labyrinth had said her name. And her message all but confirms that there may be more cursed people on her farm.

A chilly breeze blows into the room, raising goosebumps on my arm.

When I shut the laptop, Nev is standing over me.

A yelp escapes from my lungs.

Nev chuckles, basking in my fear. "So, have you finally connected the dots?"

"What do you want?" I ask.

"Merely checking your progress." Nev looks at her fingernails. "That was some performance you gave yesterday. Music is the *universal language that brings worlds together,* hmm? Well, your time is running dangerously thin, and frankly, I'm on the edge of my seat. Music won't break your curse. Tell me, are you any closer to finding true love than you were on your wedding day?"

I look away. A young lady did tell me she loved me yesterday. She even said it was true love, but nothing happened. The truth is, I'm no closer to love than I was before. Maybe Nev knows how close I came to giving up yesterday. I had opened my mouth, ready to say the magic words and go back to Veron. But the music had stopped me.

I look at the guitar Danny gave to me—its smooth wood and tight strings constructing a magic so much more intricate than its parts. With this magic, he found true love. He started a family. And last night, he gave that magic to me.

The guitar was once the most important treasure in his life. How much love does one require to give up something so important?

When I think about this, I realize maybe I *am* close. I'm not ready to give up. Danny found true love with the guitar. Maybe I can, too.

Nev smirks. "Your silence says it all. I'd get going if I were you. After all, it's almost Friday. Unless, of course, you surrender now."

I make a fist. "You wish."

The Winter Queen shrugs. "Hmm. Suit yourself. I know an excellent pumpkin pie recipe."

With a twist of her wrist, Nev vanishes in a swirl of wind that coats Isaac's windows with frost.

By the time she leaves, my blood is on fire. I stand and strike Isaac's wall with my bare knuckles. Nev will come back to taunt me before Friday, and she's untouchable. I can't move against her.

At least, not without my dagger.

I have to go to Farmer Elaine's.

Out of courtesy, I send Isaac a message through his laptop. I don't want him to worry again.

With some Belhaven currency and my new guitar, I set out for the farm by way of taxi.

Right away, I recognize Farmer Elaine from her photograph. By the knowing grin on her face, I almost wonder if she recognizes me, too. She waves her hands and gazes into her wizard's glass, then flicks a finger at me.

"You," she says. "There's something special about you. Have I seen you before, honey?"

I walk up to her, bow before her, and then rest the guitar on my toe. I've learned by now that handshakes are customary in Belhaven, but there's something different about Elaine. She seems to walk between worlds like me. "Lady Elaine," I say, "I'm pleased to meet you. A few days ago, a boy found a blue pumpkin in the haunted corn labyrinth, and you took a photograph with him."

Elaine claps her hands, her bracelets ringing with every beat. "Why, of course, I remember that beautiful pumpkin! Oh, I just knew it would be the best promotion for this farm. The *best*. Now, what about it, sweetie?"

I take a deep breath. "I am that pumpkin."

Elaine frowns. Her eyes drill into mine as if she's searching for some sort of confirmation. Then to my disappointment, she claps her hands again and lets out a full, rich belly laugh. "*You're* the blue pumpkin?" She turns to her comrades—a shepherdess in pink and a boy about my age who has painted himself to look like a skeleton. "What do you know, loves? The blue pumpkin has returned to say hello. And he plays guitar! Boy, I thought I'd seen everything by now."

The shepherdess puts a hand over her mouth and raises her crook. "Oh my," she says. "He's certainly much taller than I remember. Do you have a name, Mr. Pumpkin?"

I can see the farmers are jesting. They don't believe a word I say. "My name is Jack," I mutter.

"Jack," the skeleton says, "as in Jack-O-Lantern? That's clever. We have a lot of people take pumpkins from our farm, but never have we had one walk back to us. That's some deep, deep magic right there."

"Yes, indeed," Elaine says. "The kind of magic you can only find at Farmer Elaine's! I swear, miracles do happen every day."

"You don't believe me," I say.

The shepherdess frowns. "Why wouldn't we? You look exactly the same."

The trio bursts into laughter, Elaine kicking

her feet under her table.

I want to take my guitar and smash her wizard's glass. Clearly, it hasn't served her well. If only I could sleep on command, I'd show them all how wrong they are. The good news is that if none of them believe me, then perhaps they aren't allies of the Winter Queen after all. They aren't holding prisoners for Nev. After all, they did let Isaac take me home.

Unless they're pretending not to believe me so I won't suspect their alliance.

But I don't have time to learn their true loyalties. There are better ways to spend my time here.

The skeleton points to my guitar. "You gonna give us a concert, Mr. O'Lantern?"

"It's Jack," I say, "and no. I'm here to find more like me. Are there others?"

"Other pumpkins?" Elaine grins. "Thousands, hon. And I'm sure they'd all be happy to see you thriving!"

"Can you show me to them?"

"For five dollars," Elaine says.

Now that I understand Belhaven currency, I count out five crisp dollar bills for Farmer Elaine. She tucks them into a metal box and points the way, past the barn doors and far into the field. She also tells me about the free hayrides and entrance to the corn labyrinth. Stars and gods, I don't *dare* return to the corn labyrinth, not with Nev watching my every move. What if she rewrites the curse again?

On my way through the festival, a man in a tent stops me. "Hey, you! You look like a real sharpshooter. You think you can pop five balloons with five darts? Win a free pumpkin?"

I grin, pay the man a dollar, and destroy five balloons—with my eyes closed.

Child stuff. This was one of my very first lessons with Samuel—only he had me throwing knives at targets painted on hay bales.

"Wow, hot shot!" The man tears me a pink ticket with a star on it. "Go out and pick your pumpkin. You can give this to Elaine on your way out."

Wicked.

I make my way to the field, where I'm instantly swallowed by a blanket of orange. Pumpkins in every direction. They go on forever, the way the ocean at home doesn't end. The way the snow looks when I stand at the curtain between Veron and Invera. And I wonder how many of these pumpkins are hiding secrets—how many of them are lost souls concealed by the Winter Queen.

"Brethren," I whisper. My lost brothers and sisters. My people. Among them, perhaps, my true love.

I wander the field, speaking to the pumpkins. "Hello?" I call. "Can any of you hear me? I'm like you. I'm the Prince of Veron, and I'm here to rescue you. Hello?"

Only the winds respond.

"Such deep sleepers," I mutter with a shake of my head.

Next, I tap on the pumpkins one by one, trying to rouse them from their cursed slumber. "Excuse me." I take a knee and bang on a particularly large, round specimen. It produces a pleasant, hollow boom like one of the drums in Isaac's music videos. Hoisting it up by its stem, I give it a shake and inspect it from top to bottom. "I don't mean to startle you, but it's urgent. Won't you please wake up? What's your name?"

Silence.

Part of me hopes it will change into Samuel or my mother. I'd even be thrilled to see the cook, Hilda.

When the pumpkin doesn't answer, I move on and repeat the process with several others. My heart soars when I find some green ones, but those are just as lifeless as the orange ones. None are blue like me.

My heart twists in my chest with every failed attempt. I suppose I should be grateful that none of these are my friends, because that means my friends might not be cursed. But it doesn't prove they're safe from Nev. It only proves that they're not here and that I've been alone from the start.

I imagine every single one of these pumpkins as a living person—someone Nev can control back home. And stars and gods, it hurts.

I have one final idea, picking up my new guitar. Danny told me this was my magic, and I wonder if maybe music really *can* break a curse.

I close my eyes and I take all this pain and loneliness, and I put it on the strings.

"Field of wonder, this is no place for a curse.

Can you hear me trying to reach you?
Field of sorrow, can't you feel my broken verse?
Can't you feel my heart turn blue?"

I don't know how to explain it, but every time I touch the guitar, it's like the words and melody spills out of some fountain deep inside. I never know they've been hiding there until they come out through my fingers and soul. And they keep coming for a while. I speak them into the air and the wind carries them somewhere I can't see. I wonder how far they'll travel.

I open my eyes.

There are people around me.

None of the pumpkins have moved, but the people are moved by the music, and so maybe this *was* magic.

The people clap, ask for photographs, and compliment my talents. "That was absolutely beautiful," an elderly woman tells me. "I felt things I haven't felt in a very long time. Thank you for that, young man."

I can't help but smile again. I feel happy when people tell me they enjoy my music. At home, I mostly played for myself. Samuel would tell me, *"If you can't play for yourself and feel something, how will anybody else feel when you play for them?"* But as the prince, the social expectation was that I be entertained by others—by magicians and jesters and lute players—not that I be the entertainer. Entertaining is a refreshing change.

But I know inherently that none of these people are my true love.

While I'm here, I find a pumpkin that I'll give to Isaac's family. Carrying both a guitar and a pumpkin at the same time is challenging, but I *do* love a challenge.

On the way out, I see the undead monstrosity and he peels his face off again. I understand now that it's been a mask all along, but I still find the act unsettling. "Hey! I recognize you," he says. "I took your fancy knife the other day. Almost took it home when you didn't claim it. I suppose you want it back, yeah?"

Something rises in my gut. "Yes, please!" I say. "Thank you, Mr. Undead, sir."

The man furrows his brows, then he escorts me to the exit and hands me back my prized dagger. It's a refreshing piece of home, made by Samuel himself.

I do miss my mentor. And my parents. And familiarity.

But I also feel a pull to Belhaven. More and more, I understand. To Isaac and his family. To pizza and taxis and strangers who enjoy music.

Walking between two worlds every day? It's strange. I let myself imagine what life would look like if I'd always been here. If this was truly home.

But it's *not* home and I don't belong here. I think that maybe I'd like to, but my curse wasn't designed that way. Nev constructed every nerve to make sure of it. To make sure I'd put down roots and feel something, only to have it all fall away to the winds of winter.

At least folks are safe here. Nev doesn't care about Belhaven. She cares about Veron, and it's my duty to make sure she doesn't touch it. It's my duty to protect it.

So, I redeem my free pumpkin, leave the farm, and I make a final decision on the way back to Isaac's house.

I won't bother looking for true love anymore. I'm not so sure it really exists other than in pizza and songs. But I do believe in duty, and I believe in everything Samuel ever taught me.

Instead of searching, I'll enjoy my final days in Belhaven. I'll play music. I'll smile. I'll laugh. I'll live a life that was never meant for me.

And on Friday night, I won't say a word about where I'm going. I'll enjoy it just like any other day. Then when Isaac and his parents go to sleep, I'll slip into the night, find a quiet place to turn, and I'll speak the magic words.

I do.

FIFTEEN

ISAAC

After a low-key school day, I come home to find Jack eating a sandwich and surfing my laptop. I can't believe it took him less than a day to become addicted to the internet. I'm not even mad. Like I said, *Galaxy's Oceans* got me in big trouble a long time ago. At least Jack is putting his time to good use watching videos of the Vegas Thunderlings, and bonus, he even knows what PB&J is now.

I toss my backpack onto the ground and go for a fist bump, a norm he caught onto quickly and with great amusement. "How was your day at the farm?" I ask.

"I brought you a gift!" He hops off my bed and yanks off one of the blankets. A dark green pumpkin sits at the foot of the bed. "Tada!"

I pick up the pumpkin. It's one of the strange ones with its twisted stem and warty surface, but that's what makes it awesome. "Yesss," I say. "Now I have one for carving! Thank you."

Jack's face goes white. "Carve?"

"That's the tradition," I say. "When you find a pumpkin for Halloween, you carve a face or a picture into it. Then you put a light inside and it glows in the dark."

"Huh." Jack strokes his chin, thinking about what he's just heard. Then a big grin spreads across his face. "Thanks for not carving me. I appreciate it."

I laugh and sit at my desk, cradling the green pumpkin in my lap. Jack's getting a pretty good handle on American humor, I think. "I knew you were special," I say. "I just didn't know how. I didn't know you were like, a person, I mean. Know what happened? My friends and I were all walking through the corn maze at Farmer Elaine's, and I wasn't watching my feet, and I guess I kicked you. I tripped, fell flat on my face, and I was all sad because my popcorn went everywhere. Did you get any popcorn today?"

Jack shakes his head. "Popcorn?"

"We'll get there," I continue. "But then I dusted myself off and turned around, and there you were. A weird blue pumpkin, half-buried in a corn field. One of a kind and perfect just as you were." I hold up Big Green. "Come to think of it, I don't know if I can carve this one, either . . .."

"That one's not a person." Jack winks and makes a pair of finger guns. "I checked. I'm sorry I tripped you, by the way."

"I'm sorry I *kicked* you."

"I didn't feel it. But I'm glad you did it. Otherwise, I would've been stuck in the corn labyrinth forever."

"It's not a very hard maze," I say. "You were right by the exit when I found you."

"That was my curse. I think it was enchanted for me to miss the exit and wander in circles." Jack takes a big, ornate knife from his belt and flips it through his fingers. "I even marked the corn husks, over and over."

I cringe. "You're, uh . . . gonna want to hide that dagger. Mom and Dad don't want any weapons in the house."

Jack tosses the blade into the air, catches it, and winces. "Sorry."

The swirls on the handle catch my eye and I hold out my hand. "Would it be cool if I look at it?"

Jack inhales deeply, releases, then holds out the dagger with both hands. "Be careful," he says. "This was a gift from my mentor and best friend, Samuel. He made it himself. It's supposed to protect me from most curses. If I ever had to slay a dragon or a vinecrawler or destroy a cursed ring? I'd always have that with me."

I touch my finger to the tip of the blade, admiring the way the metal catches the light. "It's beautiful," I say. "Are curses like, a common thing in your kingdom?"

"We can never be too careful," Jack says somberly.

"So uh . . . what's a vinecrawler?"

Jack rubs his chin, looking around my room. "May I have something to paint with? I'll show you."

I laugh, grab a pen and a notebook, and flip to an empty page for him. "You can draw it in my notebook."

Jack clicks the pen and makes a doodle, biting his lip as he creates his vinecrawler. "So, it has . . . four legs and four eyes." He draws a big X across the page, a diamond in the middle, and four circles positioned around the diamond. "It's covered in fur." He makes squiggles on each leg of the X. "And also, pincers on each leg and all under the eyes."

When he hands me back my notebook, I'm terrified. It reminds me of half a spider with about a dozen mutations. "This is horrifying."

"They're friendly!" he says lightly. "They're found in plants and they slide up and down the stem, protecting them from parasites. But sometimes they get really big, and they attack if they're bothered." He holds his hands about five feet apart, elaborating on the apparent meaning of *really big*.

I swallow air with an audible gulp. "Well, that's reassuring." I close my notebook to hide the vinecrawler. "Good thing that's not your curse."

"Agreed."

I give him back his dagger, holding it like

it might detonate if I move too fast. "You can put this in the safe box in my closet. The key's in my sock drawer. As long as you don't have it out in the open, you'll be okay."

"Wicked." Jack tosses the dagger in the air, catches it one more time, and sets it on my dresser. "Thank you. I can teach you some techniques sometime, in case you're ever cursed."

"That would be awesome. Although, we don't really have to worry about that here." I grin, and a thought hits me. "Wait a minute." I stand and scratch my head. "When I found you in the corn maze, you were already a pumpkin. And you say you were cursed to wander every night and change back during the day."

Jack stares down at his reflection in the blade, his lips tight.

"But I pulled you out." The fact that this happened about four days ago makes my head spin. There's a lot I don't know about Jack, but in a few days, he's become a fixture in my life. "So why isn't the curse broken?"

Instead of answering, Jack reaches for his half-eaten PB&J and stuffs all of it into his mouth. His cheeks bulge, and I can practically see the peanut butter gluing his mouth shut.

I wrinkle my brows and Jack just shrugs. He makes a noise in his throat that has all the intonation of *I don't know* and none of the letters.

I sigh and make my way to the door. "You need a glass of milk."

Jack gives me the thumbs up and mumbles approval through his peanut butter.

I go downstairs to pour his milk, and I can't help but be a little bit frustrated. I'm noticing a pattern with Jack. Every time I feel like I'm about to break new ground on his situation, he shuts down. He springs his own trap. I'm guessing the runaway bride and the curse are related, but I can't connect the dots. Therefore, I don't know how to help him. That's the most frustrating part of all this. I want to help Jack, I just don't know how.

I remind myself that this is his fight, and I shouldn't force him to tell me anything. He needs to do that on his own time. All I can do is create the conditions that might help him feel comfortable. Food to eat. A place to sleep. Music. A friend.

Maybe I'm wrong to leave him alone during the day. I need to give him something to do.

In the bit of time before my parents come home, I finish my homework while Jack surfs the web, falling deeper into a musical rabbit hole. There's nothing the guy doesn't love—alternative rock, pop, even a little country and folk. As he makes new discoveries, he writes down band names and even tries to pick up a few tunes on his guitar. Seriously, the dude's a natural.

Once the 'rents get home, we all pile into Dad's car. He whisks us off to the Moo Factory, currently pretending to be the *Boo* Factory.

My favorite ice cream shop has changed the names of all its flavors to be slightly less appealing for the month. I quietly explain to Jack that the Bloody Basin is really just strawberry and creme, that Spider Silk is vanilla with ribbons of chocolate syrup, and that unfortunately, I don't know what Frankenguts is supposed to be, and I don't necessarily recommend it.

But I do love me some Rocktober Road, and Jack turns out to be a big fan, too.

"Stars and gods!" he says when he has his first spoonful. "I mean, *wicked*."

Mom laughs through a mouthful of Ghoulsberry. "You like ice cream, Jack?"

Jack gives two emphatic thumbs up.

"This place has been around forever," Dad says. "I used to come here all the time in high school. Maybe we should make it a Wednesday tradition."

Hearing this, Jack slows down on his treat. Every spoonful becomes calculated and deliberate, like he wants to savor every marshmallow and almond. It's almost cute watching a sixteen-year-old enjoy ice cream for probably the first time in his life. I have to get a picture.

"WowFeed time."

Jack wows me when he holds out his hand. "Hand me your phone so we can take a selfie together."

Bless the internet and all it has taught this guy.

Jack and I do one together, opting for a too-cool-for-the camera secret agent sort of pose, and then I bring Mom and Dad into the next one, all four of us holding up our orange spoons.

I'm framing these.

Mom puts her ice cream down and wipes her mouth. "So, before we start having *too* much fun, we need to talk about something real. Can we shift gears for a moment?"

I brace myself on Jack's behalf for the *stay in school* talk, glad Mom had the decency to warn me yesterday.

Dad shifts uncomfortably and looks at his hands, and Mom takes a deep breath.

"Jack," she says. "Last night before Danny and I went to bed, we poked our heads in the door to make sure you were comfortable."

My heart sinks and my hands go cold.

They found out about the pumpkin thing. How will we ever explain this, and how have they been so casual tonight?

I grip my armrest, squeezing until all the stuffing contracts into nothing.

Dad picks up where Mom left off. "And we noticed that you weren't in bed. Instead, we found that radioactive pumpkin on the pillow, and you were nowhere in the house." He frowns like he's trying to find the right words. "Did you sneak out in the middle of the night?"

"Dad," I start to protest.

Dad holds up a hand.

"Mom—"

Mom shakes her head and points at Jack. "He's allowed to speak for himself."

Dad leans across the table and meets Jack eye to eye. "*Mijo*, we're not mad at you. We just want to understand. We want to help. If you're not comfortable at our house—"

"Yes," Jack says quietly, holding my dad's eye contact. He looks trapped again, all that bright-eyed joy falling away. "I sneak out sometimes. But I don't go far. Sometimes I just wake up in the middle of the night and then I step outside. Just for some air."

Something like relief settles in my gut because Jack has dodged the curses and wizardry of this all. Honestly, I was terrified he was going to spill the beans about his pumpkin curse thing, and I'm not sure how Mom and Dad would respond. My guess is they'd throw him out for telling what sounds like a smug, flat-out lie, or they'd have him committed somewhere.

Dad shoots his gaze to me. "Did you know?"

I nod. "I knew."

"But why?" Mom says. "It can be dangerous to walk around outside alone in those hours. I know Belhaven is small, but *lindo*, I just don't feel right about it. Can you help us understand why? Are we the problem?"

As relieved as I am about what we've dodged, I *hate* that they've thrown this spotlight on my friend. Because now the only way out is to keep lying and lying until he's no longer free from his trap—he's at the bottom of a hole. I put my ice cream down and pound a fist on the table. "Can't you be more sensitive?" I ask. "Use your heads! He's coming from a rough home. He doesn't want to be questioned about it all day."

And I'm the worst. Because just a few hours ago, I was prying, too. I slouch in my seat and cross my arms.

Jack interjects, "No. I get worried."

This doesn't sound like a half-truth at all. It's from deep within, like his music.

Mom puts a hand over her heart. "What are you worrying about?"

"My future." He pauses. "And . . . someone from home."

A tear breaks loose from Mom's eye and she quickly wipes it away. "It breaks my heart that you have these worries. You should be free to think about school and dating and having fun and . . . I don't know." She reaches out and grabs Jack's hand. "I don't know your whole story, but I promise we will keep you safe. You don't have to worry. I mean it when I say you can stay as long as you want, even if that means making you our son."

My jaw drops. I'm bewildered at how fully my parents have started to invest in Jack's well-being. They've always been nurturing to all my friends—cooking them dinner, offering them rides to places, even going so far as to "friend" them on all our social media sites and wish them happy birthday every year. That's the Costa way, I guess. Community care, through and through. What I'm seeing is their highest form of care.

Jack looks around the table and smiles at each of us in turn. "You all are very kind," he says. "You're like my lucky stars."

"Oh, don't have me in my feels." I look away.

"Would you be interested, though?" Dad

asks. "In staying and being in the family?"

Mom raises a finger. "We would ask that you go to school and that you don't sneak out at night, but we would be glad to have you. You make us so happy, and you seem so deserving of a family who cares. Again, I don't know why you left your old home or what your story is, but I just want you to know that you're welcome here. That's all."

Jack's trapped again. Maybe my parents came on too strong. I'm over the moon about their offer, and the idea of having Jack around more officially makes my heart full. It feels *right*, even if there are so many bumps to think about. This "sneaking out at night" lie won't last forever, and it hits me that Mom and Dad are almost sure to check in again tonight. And the next, and the next, until they find two boys who have established a pattern of sleeping in their own beds.

I nudge him with my elbow. "What do you think?"

Jack stares at his ice cream and runs a hand through his hair. "Um. May I please have a few days to think about it?"

"Of course," Mom whispers.

"We don't mean to impose," Dad says. "It's an open invitation."

The air lightens a bit and Jack nods. "Thank you," he says, "for the ice cream and for everything."

"You're so welcome," Mom says. "This is so nice, by the way. Isn't it fun? Just getting out and into the world sometimes? When's the last time we did this?"

Dad pats his belly. "I dunno, but I'm ready for a movie."

From malls to movie theaters, Jack's really getting the crash course in American culture this week.

I introduce him to popcorn, which he doesn't love, but he's amazed by the enormous screen and the wall of sound.

Mom and Dad pick the movie, and it all goes over my head. There's enough action and explosions to keep me staring, but I understand none of the plot.

So, I'm not entirely surprised to find Jack nodding off toward the end of the movie.

His eyelids droop shut and his chin dips toward his chest. Down, down, down, and then he snaps back up again, fully alert.

My heart kicks into overdrive. All I need right now is for Jack to Hulk out into a vegetable in a crowded movie theater.

He droops again.

"Hey," I whisper. "Don't you sleep."

This buys me a few minutes before Jack goes back down.

I stomp on his toes and rouse him back to life. This time, he's alert enough to laugh at one of the jokes in the movie.

Just before the credits roll, I hear a single snore. When I turn my head, the blue pumpkin is sitting in Jack's seat. I wail on it with my fists until my friend pops back out, completing his transformation just in time for my parents to look over.

"You guys like that?" Dad asks.

"That was heart-pounding!" Mom raises one hand way over her head. "My pulse is all the way up here!"

"Yeah, Ma," I say. "Mine, too."

Jack springs to his feet. "That was sick!" He claps, initiating a round of applause through the auditorium.

My adrenaline's still pumping when we all file out of the theater together. Maybe trying to keep Jack awake has me super alert or something, but something else puts me on edge. Just after Jack bolts to the restroom, a woman in a white and silver gown emerges from the lady's room, and something about her icy expression really bothers me. She sips on a cherry FrostiFreeze, and tiny metal snowflakes dangle from rods in her hair. She stares right at me as she saunters toward the exit, almost in slow motion.

I rub down the goosebumps on my arm, unsure if I'm cold or freaked out, or both.

But hey, it's Halloween season, the time of chills and thrills.

Obviously, it's nothing.

THURSDAY, OCTOBER 30

THE CURSE OF FAME

SIXTEEN

JACK

Today, I get to go to school with Isaac!

I've replaced my boots with some fancy new shoes, and I've agreed to a few things. I should try not to say *stars and gods* when I'm excited. I don't have to let Isaac do *all* the talking—just most of it. I shouldn't raise my hand in class or even really participate, unless I'm called on, and under no circumstances am I to go looking for dragons.

"If you see a fluffy dragon walking around," Isaac says, "it's not real. It's a student in a costume, like the people in the movies. So don't attack and don't be weird, cool?"

"Me? Weird?" I say.

Isaac narrows his eyes.

"I jest. I understand."

This is essentially my last full day in Belhaven—my last full cycle of living this strange life, staying up late, and knowing that I'll wake up in Isaac's room tomorrow. But my heart is full because when I leave this town and go back home, I'll have so many stories to take back to my old life. I'll get to talk about high school and movie theaters and Rocktober Road, and know that I lived my short time in Belhaven as fully as possible.

When I go back home, I won't be living my old life *or* this life. I'll be a married prince fighting the Winter Queen and trying to protect her daughter and citizens. I'll need all the strength I can get. I'll need happy memories to draw on. I'll need reminders that there are lovely things and people worth fighting for.

Danny and Diana *almost* changed my mind last night about going home. Their loving offer to make me a part of their family nearly brought tears to my eyes. I'll never forget it.

And it's also because of their affection that I can't accept their offer.

When I told them I was worried about

someone from home, that was only half of the truth. Sure, Nev *will* come after me, and I'll be waiting. I have my dagger back. I have all I've learned from Samuel.

But I can't risk the Costas getting hurt. Not Isaac.

Every day, he moves closer to uncovering my story. I had to shove a sandwich into my mouth yesterday to protect that story. Every night, he and his family grow closer to me, and I grow closer to them. If I stay here, I'll just become a vegetable by Saturday, and then the Costas will be Nev's targets. She'll fill their house with Winter's Bite, and they won't survive.

I can hardly bear the idea.

But at least we have today.

"Remember, you're just Jack from out of town." Isaac hands me my visitor pass. "And you're staying with my family for a while, and if people really start prying about your past, you're from Arizona. It's always summery enough that anything you say about home will make sense. Got it?"

I give him the thumbs up. "Got it, dude."

"Now you're catching on! Come on, we have

bio. And don't you dare fall asleep in class."

To make sure of this, Isaac has introduced me to a potion called *cold brew*. Lightning runs through my veins, and I feel as though I'll sprout wings at any moment.

"Welcome, Mr. Zuka." Isaac's teacher, Mrs. McKelvey, shakes my hand. "You picked a great day to join us. Today we're doing the cheese lab and witnessing the power of enzymes in action. You and Mr. Costa can partner up. Do you like cheese?"

"Oh yes," I say, "especially on pizza. Pizza's my true love."

Mrs. McKelvey laughs. "Isn't it all of ours?" She shakes a red box marked *Bitz*. "I don't have pizza today, but we do have crackers! Hope you're hungry."

Science is more difficult in Belhaven. Back home, Samuel would show me diagrams of space, and sometimes we'd go up to an observatory and look at the stars. The lesson was always that space is very big, that it's always moving, and that as far as we know, the sun and everything else in the universe revolve around our land, which is flat like a pizza.

I don't understand enzymes, but I help Isaac as much as I can. I measure milk and hold the cloth in place after he adds the enzymes, and I have the most fun straining out the liquids and watching the cheese appear as if by sorcery. The lesson I learn is that science *is* sorcery, and that it can be tasty on crackers. This is what I tell Mrs. McKelvey when she approaches me at the end of the class and asks what I think of Belhaven biology.

"Cheers to that!" she tells me. "Science *is* tasty. That's why I became a teacher. You're welcome in my classroom any day."

I despise math. At home, we count, we add, and we subtract. I don't understand why Belhaven puts letters and numbers together. The lesson goes over my head, but Isaac's math teacher commends me on being a polite young man.

English is awesome. The teacher, Mrs. Cruze, invites me to join the class in freewriting for the day, which is cathartic and liberating. "Just write whatever's on your heart right now, and then you get to keep it. Freewriting is just for you."

And there's a lot on my heart today, so it

feels nice to let it out. In fact, something about freewriting seems to change me. I feel lighter somehow. I didn't know I had all these words—and thoughts and feelings—inside of me until they spilled onto the paper.

At the end of class, I tell Mrs. Cruze that I enjoyed freewriting.

"I enjoyed having you!" she says. "And if you do this often, you can look back one day and reread these and see how you've grown. Keep it up!"

On the way to lunch, Isaac gives me a fist bump. I still love fist bumps. There's something gratifying about crashing knuckles together for joy and endearment.

"You're kind of a teacher's pet," he says. "I mean, I am too, but my teachers *love* you! You have to enroll here."

I feel my face go red and run a hand through my hair. "Love? Nah."

We're walking to a table to eat when a tall boy steps into our path.

"Isaac," he says.

Isaac freezes, and I can see the sweat glistening on his forehead. "Seth. Hi."

"Hi." The tall boy crams his hands into his

pockets, bouncing on the balls of his feet. "It's, uh . . . been a little while. Been thinking about ya and just wanted to see how you're doing."

"I'm fine," Isaac says. "Yeah. Everything's good. Nice of you to care."

"Well, I always did, so . . .." The boy cuts his eyes to me and looks me up and down. "Who's this?"

I don't like him.

Regardless, we shake hands.

"This is my friend Jack," Isaac says. "He's from out of town."

"Seth." The boy eyes my visitor pass, rubbing his chin. "Interesting. Jack from out of town, hm? Where out of town?"

"Arizona," I say.

Seth cringes. "Oof. I'm sorry. Is it really a dry heat like they say?"

"Sure," I answer. "Always summer."

"Heh." Seth points to me. "I like this guy. Did you ever catch that dragon, by the way? We need more people like you on the lookout. Wouldn't want some loose monster destroying the school, especially not before the Fall Ball."

"God, Seth." Isaac rolls his eyes. "Are you

done yet? Can I eat lunch with my friend now?"

This is a different Isaac. Something about Seth changes him, but I can't understand how. I think Seth might be an enzyme.

Seth's hands go back into his pockets. "Sure, sure. Just remember that I was your friend, too. And by the way, it's all *your* fault Sun broke up with me."

Seth walks away, boot heels pounding on tile.

When Isaac looks at me, his face is ghost white and his eyes are brimming with tears. He lets out a deep breath. "Can we go eat somewhere else, please?"

"I'm following you today," I say. "Wherever you want to go."

Without a word, Isaac brushes his face with a sleeve and carries his lunch out of the cafeteria. I follow him to the drama building, where we sit against a brick wall and Isaac unpacks his lunch. There's no one else around, and it's the most silence I've heard all day.

After he finishes a bite of his pizza, Isaac clears his throat and nudges me with an elbow. "I'm sorry about that," he says. "Seth and I have a kind of history. I thought I had moved on, but I didn't expect to have that conversation with him right now."

I think about the first night I met Isaac. There was a moment where I felt like he'd been touched by the Winter Queen, frozen in his bed and talking about his pain. A thought enters my mind, but it takes some courage to ask.

"Isaac," I say slowly, "is Seth the one who caused your heartbreak?"

Isaac takes a deep breath, but he doesn't look me in the eye. "Yes."

"Because he was your friend?"

"Because he was *everything*. Yes, heartbreak can happen between friends, but with me and Seth, it was more."

I rub my chin. "More? Like love?"

Isaac shrugs. "I don't know anymore. Maybe. Probably the closest I've ever been at least."

"Did your parents pick him?" I ask. "For betrothal?"

A smile flickers on Isaac's face, then disappears when he shakes his head. "No, you goof. We picked each other. My parents liked him, though. He's hard not to like if you really know him. And no, we were never 'betrothed.' Here, people wait for that. Usually until after high school."

"Huh." I stare into the distance, iron clouds gathering over the purple mountains, and I think for a minute. "I'm sorry, Isaac."

My friend fidgets with his shoelace. "Does it bother you? What I just told you?"

"Yes," I said. "It makes me sad that he broke your heart."

"But like, you don't care that I fell in love with a *dude*?" Isaac asks. "Because sometimes people have issues with that. I don't know what it's like in, uh, Veron or wherever. If you're not cool with it or if you think it's wrong, then um . . ." he trails off and pulls his knees up to his chest. In the moment, he looks smaller than he really is. But I know he's grander. Mightier. Even more than I realized before.

I pull him into one of those buddy hugs he's done with me before. "Where I'm from, royal families choose our marriages for us. They tell us who to fall in love with, and they match us to draw new boundaries for the kingdom." I take a deep breath. "I met Aurora on our wedding day. But stars and gods, people should be allowed to love whoever they love! They should be allowed to have their hearts broken by whoever they want to give them to. A prince or a princess, a farmer, a friend. Man or woman or anyone. My mentor says sharing your heart with someone is the bravest thing anyone can do. I'm sorry that yours was broken, but I think you were still brave to share it with Seth."

In my home kingdom, these royal matches are always between man and woman because they want to produce heirs. So, I've never seen love any other way. In fact, I'm still not sure if I know what it is. One day I asked Samuel, and he told me that love is a meeting of the stars. That it's like sunlight filling you from your head to toe. Maybe that's why legends talk about Summer's Glow. Whatever love is, why should it be any different between two men or between two women or any combination of human beings?

Love should just be love. The end.

Some silence passes between Isaac and I

before he says, "Yeah. Maybe that was brave. It hurts, but it was worth it. Thank you for accepting my whole self."

This time, I initiate the fist bump. "I like your whole self." I remember his words from yesterday. "One of a kind and perfect just as you are. My friend."

Isaac lights up. There's something about that big smile that makes my heart feel full, but there's also something about it that empties me this time. It's knowing that tomorrow is my last day with Isaac, and the fact that friends can break each other's hearts, too. I'm worried that leaving might hurt him again.

But at least leaving will keep him safe.

"There you are!" A girl steps into our view, takes Isaac by the hand, and says, "Now that I've broken up with Seth, can we all go to the Fall Ball together tomorrow? Please?"

"Sun," Isaac says, "you shouldn't have done that. I told you not to break up with him."

"It was my decision," the girl says. "We didn't even click. It was always weird."

She turns to me, extends her hand, and says, "You must be Jack. Will you please accompany all of us to the Fall Ball tomorrow night? It'll be loads of fun, and it's the best way to spend Halloween night—among friends and loved ones. Oh, I'm Sun, by the way."

Isaac buries his hand in his hair. "You know you've actually made things worse. Seth's mad at me. It's gonna be so awkward now. There's no way I'm going to the Fall Ball, especially not now."

"He will get over it," Sun says. "I'll work some Halloween magic. I just want all of us together again."

A celebration of autumn. The *perfect* way to spend my final hours in Belhaven.

"I'd like to go," I say. "To the Fall Ball tomorrow."

Isaac's eyes go wide and his mouth falls open. "Wait, you do? You seriously wanna go?"

Sun jumps up and down. "Yes! He wants to go. You are hereby obligated, Isaac Costa. Who are you to deny your friends the best night ever?"

"Yes," I say more forcefully, "I really want to go!"

Isaac laughs. "All right," he says. "Fine. I guess we're going to the Fall Ball. But if Seth pulls anything and the night gets weird, Jack and I are out. Got it?"

"Fine, fine, I guarantee you there will be no Seth weirdness." Sun waves her hand in front of her face like she's swatting at a fly. "So . . . it's a date! A group date. Miranda's gonna be so excited. I hope you both have costumes. Warm costumes, because it's still supposed to storm tomorrow."

"Blah," Isaac says. "Jack, you wanna go shopping later? I guess we have a date tomorrow. A *group* date."

"A group date." *Huh.* "Sounds wicked."

SEVENTEEN

ISAAC

By seventh period Spanish, I was terrified Jack would crumple under a sugar crash. For a couple of weeks, our teacher was having us research a Spanish-speaking country of our choice, and today we started presenting our findings. I gave a PowerPoint on Spain, and I kept thinking, *Jack, please don't get bored and crash out*. I juiced him up this morning with a sugary vanilla cold brew, and his knee was bouncing all through bio. His hands jittered like they were full of crickets. The fact that we finished the cheese lab without him dumping our whole experiment down the drain? Now *that* was a Halloween miracle.

The Spanish presentation made me

especially nervous because Jack doesn't know a word of it. But I saw him lean forward, resting his chin on his hands and staring at all the pictures I'd selected of Madrid, Granada, and Barcelona. Jack's innocent state of constant wonderment turned out to be just the encouragement I needed.

After school, Jack and I walk down to the Stardust Costume Shop. On the way over, Jack says, "Can we go to the place from your presentation after this?"

I draw a blank. "Huh?"

"España," Jack says. "It seems so beautiful. Let's go run with the *toros* in the streets. Or in the arenas. It seems so exciting! Have you done it before?"

I grin. He's thinking of the traditional running of the bulls in Pamplona, which I showed a video clip for on my PowerPoint. Every year around the summertime, they host the San Fermin festival. They fence off a section of the streets and set up a route to an arena, where *matadores* and bulls will fight in front of a crowd. But first, the bulls run loose in the streets, and so do the humans. Some of the humans get trampled or gored every year.

And like, I always thought Black Friday shopping was chaos.

Still, I crack up. "No, Jack. I haven't run or fought with bulls before. Not everyone's an adrenaline-junkie like you. You were ready to fight a dragon the other day. Or a vinecrawler." I point to a white costume with notes of red. "But hey, you could be a matador at the Fall Ball tomorrow if you wanted."

"What about in España?"

"We can't just go to Spain today," I say. "It's on the other side of the world, my dude. We'd have to save up a ton of money first, buy plane tickets, and then fly over the ocean for at least twelve hours."

Jack snaps his fingers. "Aw, man."

"I know, right? You'd probably enjoy the Belhaven rodeo, though. I don't love it, but I bet you'd find it exciting. There's a big parade, and then people actually ride the bulls. We'd just have to wait until February. Four months. It's not that far away."

Jack picks up a bottle of fake blood and gives it a half-hearted shake. "Yeah. That would be fun."

I still can't believe Jack talked me into going

tomorrow. Why did Sun have to open her big mouth? *Curse you, Sun.*

"What kind of costume do you want?" I ask. "Try some on. The cool thing is you can be anything you want on Halloween. Endless possibilities. At least, as many as there are in this store."

The vast selection is almost too much for Jack to wrap his head around. His pop culture knowledge is limited to a series of five-minute highlight reels I found on the internet, so he doesn't get excited about things like Disney characters. Yet. This is just a gap I need to fill for him.

I suggest a few superheroes, thinking he might like their backstories.

"This guy's a classic." I hand him a star-spangled costume that looks about his size. "Basically, he took a potion that turned him into a super soldier, and he's all about justice and all that good stuff. And," I reach for a flimsy plastic disc on the display, "his shield is made of a crazy strong metal that nobody can cut through. Plus, it kind of works like a boomerang. He can whip it around and hit a bunch of baddies, and it always comes back to him no matter how far he throws it. Try it on."

"*Nice.*" Jack takes the costume and the shield, then disappears behind a curtain.

He emerges in the outfit a few minutes later, a look of pride gleaming in his eyes.

"How do you feel?" I ask.

"Like a super soldier."

To my horror, Jack twists to the side, curls back his arm, and flings the shield as hard as he can. Time expands into slow motion as the shield whirls over the sales floor, and I do some mental calculus to guess where it will land. The store's a little crowded with people who waited to pick costumes until the last minute, like me. The odds are ten to one that the shield will smack somebody.

"*Nooo,*" I bellow.

The shield connects with an animatronic statue of Freddy Krueger, barely makes a sound, and then flitters down to the floor. The motion triggers Freddy to wiggle his fingers in his razor glove, and a recording of his laugh plays. "*I'll see you in your nightmares!*"

"Excuse me!" A shop worker wags her finger at Jack. "You can't throw things."

Jack scratches his head through his rubber

helmet. "The shield doesn't work. I don't feel so super."

Turning red, I shuffle across the floor to pick up the shield. Freddy informs me yet again that he'll see me in my nightmares. He must be getting tired of repeating this because his voice crackles with static. His batteries will die any minute.

I hang up the shield and select another superhero for Jack.

"Let's try again. Maybe you can be the Caped Crusader. With this costume, you wouldn't need a prop." I drop my voice to a husky, raspy tone. "We can just work on getting you to sound like this because that's how he talks. He has all these cool gadgets and inspires fear in the criminals of the city."

Jack clears his throat, narrows his eyes, and says in a perfect imitation of the voice, "Isaac. I saw this on the internet yesterday. I love bats."

I clap my hands. "Dang, you're pretty good at that! My throat hurts just from talking like that for two seconds. Go try it on."

He disappears behind the curtain and when he returns, I'm floored. Jack makes a good Caped Crusader. I think it's the height and the way he's built, which almost makes up for all the cheap padding in the chest and shoulders of the costume. He also has the chin, which is one of the Dark Knight's most underrated features.

Jack gives me this broody face, eyes of stone, and puts his hands on his hips. "I have a problem," he says in the Dark Knight's voice. "This cowl feels very tight and unpleasant."

"Ihatetobreakittoyou,man,butdiscomfort's part of the territory on Halloween. There are good costumes, and there are comfortable costumes. Unfortunately, they're almost never the same." For the first time, I look at the price tag for the Crusader, and my heart skips a beat. "Actually, you're right. Let's scale back to something comfortable."

I curate some classics for Jack—a blend of spooky, practical, magical, historical, and anything that catches his eye. I draw from this same selection, too, and time flies while Jack and I try on different costumes. We become wizards, which he finds comfortable but uninspiring. I scale up. We try ghouls and vampires, which he finds fascinating but unsettling. Wonder if they make him hyperaware of his curse. I steer away from the horror theme.

I think we've finally found a winner in the cowboy costumes until he whips off his hat, spins it on his finger, and says, "I think I want to be a prince tomorrow."

The solution is so simple and obvious that I can't believe we've been missing it this whole time. He already has everything he needs for a costume, yet everybody at the Fall Ball will assume he went out of his way to pull it all together. They won't blink twice, yet they'll be floored at the authenticity. For the first time, he'll blend in by being exactly who he is.

"Are you sure? I mean, it makes all the sense in the world, but tomorrow's also a fun day to be someone you're not. Do you want to try something else?" I grab a black, tattered vest decked out with skulls and crossbones. "Let's be pirates!"

Jack shakes his head. "Going as the prince will be perfect then, because lately, I don't feel like Prince Jack. I feel like I'm becoming a different Jack now." He stares into his cowboy hat, then returns it to its rack. He eyes his reflection in a cheap plastic crown. "I wonder if I try on Prince Jack again, will I feel like I'm pretending? Or will I feel real?"

I let my friend wander in his head for a minute, wishing more than anything that I could take a peek inside. His mind must be a beehive, buzzing with activity in a million tiny compartments. Careful not to startle him out of his thoughts, I rest my hand on his shoulder.

A pang of guilt stabs me in the gut when I think of our earliest days together. I wonder if I've been confusing him, trying to sculpt him into some teenage American drone like all the rest of us. *Don't be weird. Nobody says stars and gods, Jack. Don't say a word and just let me do all the talking. We need to get you some new shoes. Study all these videos so you can learn how to be just like the rest of us.*

This trap that I keep seeing when Jack gets all quiet like this?

It's me.

I'm ruining him by trying to make him normal.

And after all he said the other day about his kingdom trying to sculpt him into the perfect prince? A real man?

This has to drive him bananas.

Before I can stop myself, both my arms are around him in a tight hug. He's stiff and motionless for a second, caught by surprise, I think. It occurs to me that I've never given Jack a real, full-bodied hug before. We've been keeping it to one-armed buddy hugs and fist bumps. My mom hugged him the day we moved him into our house, and I know he really liked that. People should be able to hug more freely. It's like medicine.

"Jack," I say. "I want you to know that you can be *whoever* you want to be, any time. You can be Prince Jack, you can be Cowboy Jack, you can be High School Jack, or whatever makes you happy. Even when Halloween is over. Okay? I won't try to make you be anything else."

This is when Jack leans into the hug and returns it. "Thank you, my friend."

I don't know why I'm surprised to feel his heartbeat, all steady and constant warmth. As goofy as it sounds, the curse thing made me question whether he'd even have a heart. I know he bleeds, but when he's a pumpkin, he's hollow, right? Just guts and seeds. Where does the heart go?

It doesn't matter. Jack is more real than any of the drones of Belhaven, even if he doesn't know it yet.

"D'aw!" A voice cuts off my thoughts, and I look up to see our student count-sil president, Jennifer Tate, observing our hug. She puts a hand to her heart. "That is so sweet. I am always here for a good bromance."

Jack and I let each other go, and I clear my throat. "Sup, Jen?"

Jennifer goes straight for Jack. "You're gonna be our performer tomorrow!" she says. "You *are* coming to the Fall Ball, right?"

I blink and shake my head. "Wait a minute, I thought you all booked Phil vs. the Specters? Aren't they playing?"

"They're stranded in L.A. Can you believe it? All sorts of flights are being cancelled because of weather right now. You'd think L.A. would be the last place to get a blizzard, but I guess anything can happen in the spooky season. Especially when I'm trying to plan the first ever Halloween dance for Belhaven." Jennifer throws her arms up in resignation. "I literally just got off the phone with them about five minutes ago, otherwise I'd be anywhere but here looking at costumes. I was trying to keep my cool, and then I saw you."

Jack's grinning like he just won a lifetime of pizza. "You want me to perform at the ball?"

"Please?" Jennifer says. "No pressure, but you're kind of my last hope. I noticed you're trending on WowFeed from when you were playing at the mall, and honestly, people would love you. I have a few other backup musicians ready to go. One even has some music written out and a possible set list. We just need somebody who can sing and play guitar." She presses her palms together like she's praying.

Feeling protective, I almost caution Jack against this. I just got done telling him he can be whatever he wants to be, and now he's being coerced into becoming Jennifer's star. Plus, setting him up for a gig the day before doesn't seem fair. How could a band be ready in time?

"StuCo will pay you," Jennifer says. "The only thing is the band wants to rehearse at five tonight, but seeing as how you're my last hope, I'm sure they can bend a little bit on the hour. I'm told they're ordering pizza."

I'm sold now. Pizza, a chance to practice, and Jack gets to do something he loves.

"Wow!" I say. "You should do it, buddy."

"Pizza?" A grin spreads across Jack's face. "I was already in before you said pizza. Sign me up!"

"Oh my god, you are the best." Jennifer pretends to fling some sweat off her forehead. "Crisis averted. Should I call the backup band and tell them you'll meet them at five? They'll be at the school. Just bring your guitar."

Jack confirms, and Jennifer breathes a thank you to the sky. She begins to make a call, forming a thumbs-up as she walks away from us. "I owe you. I owe you big time. Yes!"

I join Jack in a goofy celebratory dance. "Check you out, rock star! You have a real gig. How does it feel?"

"It feels . . . .." Jack looks back at his reflection, standing taller. "It feels real."

"You're gonna blow this whole town away tomorrow," I say. "I'll walk you to the school at five. I'm so excited. You're gonna crush it."

And he is.

Nothing can stand in his way.

EIGHTEEN

JACK

After taking an hour or so to rest, Isaac walks me to rehearsal, and he is glowing. In fact, he trots like a steed the whole way.

"So, get this!" Isaac reads his smartphone while he walks. "I've told you about Miranda, right? She's one of my best friends, and she plays bass guitar. She just texted me and it turns out she's one of the musicians Jennifer tapped to play with you tomorrow. I have *two* friends in the band tomorrow, and I can't stop talking about it!" He turns in a full circle, fists in the air. "I mean, six or seven hours ago I was determined not to go to the Fall Ball at all, and now I get to say I'm with the band. Do you know how much I've always wanted to say, 'I'm with the band'? A *lot*."

Isaac jumps in the air and kicks his heels together.

"Isaac, calm down," I say with a chuckle. "You haven't even had any coffee."

"This feeling is better than coffee. Everything is perfect, and nothing can ruin my day." He freezes, one foot hovering over the sidewalk. "Wait. If you're in the band, and Miranda's in the band, then that means Armand and I are stuck with Seth and Sun. Oh man, what if they turn into drama llamas, Jack?"

I nudge him forward. "Come *on*, Isaac. Don't let yourself be the drama llama."

He lights up again. "True. It's all good, and do you know why? 'Cause I'm with the band!"

"I'm not worthy of all this praise," I say. "I'm not Chris D'Agosto. I'm just Jack. Remember?"

"Hang on. Nobody's Chris D'Agosto." Isaac holds up one finger. "But my parents would beg to differ with you. Did you hear how excited they were that you're playing tomorrow? You haven't even had that guitar for a week, and you've already scored a gig. It's like my dad told you, it's your magic. Pretty sure they're relieved I'm going, too. They get all smothery when they think I'm lonely. Only now, everything feels perfect. Y'know?"

Something icy grips my chest. My fingers become sweaty, and the guitar case grows heavy. This is guilt. I don't think I deserve this guitar, or this show, or all this praise.

I'm leaving tomorrow.

"Speaking of my parents," Isaac says. "Did you get to think some more about their offer from last night? You know, to make you a part of the family?"

"Not yet." The guilt monster grows. I also lied to Danny and Diana last night about sneaking out of the house. And then, Isaac helped me keep lying by stuffing his bedsheets with the pumpkin he named Big Green, and with a bunch of other items that add up to the shape of me, just in case they checked again. "It's, uh . . . been a busy day. I haven't had a lot of time to think about it."

Isaac nods. "I get it. I don't want to rush you. But you're right. It's been an *awesome* day. This school fits you better than I thought it would. Knowing my mom, she'll probably have you enrolling by Monday. She lives and breathes school. It's like her whole thing.

She's all about getting me a scholarship and eventually out of Belhaven."

I pause. "Out of Belhaven?"

"Mm-hmm. I think my parents always wanted to get out, but they got a nice big house and put all their energy into getting me out. I know I'm lucky my parents care so much, but I still have all of high school ahead of me."

Something about this topic is bittersweet to me. I'll probably never find a way to come back to Belhaven. It never occurred to me that if I do find a way to return, Isaac may not be here. And I want to remember all this the way it is. I can't picture Belhaven without Isaac, or Isaac outside of Belhaven.

But there are other kingdoms for him to explore. He deserves to enjoy his adventures as much as I'm enjoying mine.

"How many other kingdoms are there besides Belhaven?" I ask. "Where would you go?"

"Oh boy, how do I even answer that?" Isaac claps a hand to his forehead. "There are probably a billion places to live in this world. I'll show you a globe when we get home. For me, I think about New York. Boston. L.A. Big cities full of adventures. Sometimes, I think about closing my eyes and throwing three darts at a map and visiting all the places that stick. Like leaving it all up to fate. But I'd also be happy staying close to home, too. Like I said, I still have all of high school ahead to figure it out. Who even knows what'll happen tomorrow?"

I strengthen my grip on the guitar case. "Yeah," I say. "Who knows?"

A frigid gust of wind rakes through my hair, and I glance around the streets. The clouds gather in droves, dark and ominous.

In spite of the weather, Isaac is more chipper than ever, and I envy his positivity. He tilts his head toward the school gates. "Well, here we are, my friend. You should get inside and meet Jennifer."

I take a deep breath, my palms suddenly slick with sweat. "You think they'll like me?"

"C'mon, they'll love you. You're perfect for this. Just go in and rock it."

Rock it. I like the sound of that.

We do our classic fist bump.

"Do you know the way home? Or I can

come back for you later?"

"I remember the way," I say.

"Sweet. Have fun, then." Isaac turns and makes his way down the street. Before he can get out of earshot, I surprise myself by opening my mouth.

"Hey, Isaac?"

My friend stops and spins around on his heel.

I look down at my toes. "I . . . don't have a lot of time left."

The words fall out slowly, and once they're gone, I wish I could take them back. The worry on Isaac's face reminds me of his heartbreak.

He takes three slow steps toward me, then freezes. "What do you mean?"

I choose my words carefully because I know Nev is listening somewhere. I just want Isaac to be prepared for me to leave Belhaven. One day, he's going to leave, too. If I come back, he won't be here. He needs to know. "The curse will end soon," I say. "When it does, I won't be here anymore."

Isaac closes the gap between us, his hands in his pockets. "How soon do you mean?"

I tighten my lips. I've already said too much, and time is strange. Already, the big green pumpkin I found for Isaac isn't quite the same as it was yesterday. Maybe I'm not the same as I was yesterday, either. Maybe nothing is ever the same from moment to moment. Again, time feels like water in my hands, always dripping through my fingers, carving up the Earth. I can't just hold onto it, even if I try to freeze it. Time is always moving.

"You don't have enough time to go to Spain and run with the bulls, do you?" Isaac asks.

I shake my head.

Isaac crosses his arms. "What about Wednesday ice cream nights?" He looks to the school gates. "Are you ever enrolling here?"

I turn away. "No."

"So, what happens when your curse is over?" Isaac's voice goes soft, barely above a whisper. "You just go home, right?"

"Yes," I say. "That's one thing that can happen."

"Or . . .? Is there another thing that can happen?"

"Yes. I become a pumpkin forever. Or as long as a pumpkin lasts before I go with the

Gray Lady."

"Gray Lady?" Isaac's eyes widen, and he pauses while the Gray Lady's name fades into the breeze. "In other words, you . . .."

Die. We don't say it. But I nod. "Yes."

Isaac looks at his shoes, and it's the saddest I've ever seen him. I'm like Seth. An enzyme. A heartbreaker. "So, how do we break this thing?"

"I . . . I can't tell you that."

"But you know how?"

I say nothing.

All at once, Isaac explodes. "Why do you keep shutting me out, then? You're not letting me help you!" Isaac's eyes fill with tears again. "Just help me understand it, and I'll do whatever I can to help you break the curse. I'll help you fight a vinecrawler, or whatever. If you have to go home, I understand. You have another life somewhere, and it's not like I thought you were gonna live with us forever." He fidgets with the zipper on his jacket. "I just don't want you to die. I know we only met a few days ago, but if something bad happened to you, it . . .."

A frigid gust of wind rakes through my air

and I tighten my lips. I can't say a word. Nev's watching. This is *her* storm. She reminded me how fast the weather can change, and now she's proving it.

"I can't say more," I say. "You don't understand, Isaac."

"I don't?" Isaac swallows. "You know, I told you one of the most difficult things I've ever had to say today. And you were actually one of the easier ones to tell. Every time I get close to someone, I have to come out all over again. The world makes us do that if we want to be who we are. I thought since I told you that today, that our friendship was real. I thought maybe we could tell each other anything. Only now I'm not so sure, because you won't tell me how to help break the curse, and it's all I want to do."

Tears and cold air prickle my eyes. "Isaac," I say. "You can't help me with this. In fact, you could get hurt."

"This already hurts," Isaac says. "What if you think of this as helping *me*? Would that make you want to tell?"

I turn away, unable to face the pain in Isaac's eyes. "No."

Isaac sniffles, turns on his heel, and makes his way down the street. "Fine. I'm gonna do my homework at Armand's. I'll probably just stay the night there. See you tomorrow or never or whatev. I even don't care anymore."

"Oh, you don't care anymore?" I call after him. If I thought he actually meant it, I wonder if I'd understand heartbreak. But I don't think he means it at all. "Wicked!"

"No, I don't care." Isaac throws his hands in the air. "Because you know what else? Forget everything I told you in the costume shop. You're *weird*. You have embarrassed me so many times this week. Throwing things at Freddy Krueger, falling asleep at the movies, storming the cafeteria to slay our mascot, becoming the teacher's pet after only one day, and the way you talk? You're a joke. Grow up and get over yourself."

The knife wound on my chest prickles me again. Before I can answer Isaac, he pulls a pair of headphones from his pocket and shoves them into his ears as he walks away. I suppose that's so he can't hear anything else I have to say. He's ended the conversation.

Stars and gods. For the first time, I'm angry

at Isaac. He understands nothing.

I turn and slam my guitar case against the school gate, my breaths shallow and hot.

At least now it'll be easier to leave Belhaven tomorrow. To say *I do* and slip away forever. Apparently, Isaac won't care, and I'd even say the words right now if I weren't so excited to perform tomorrow.

Because Isaac was wrong. When I go back to Veron, I *can't* be anything I want. I have to be Prince Jack, whether I feel like him or not. I have to be what the kingdom shapes me to be and move when they pull their strings. Marry the princess. Take the throne. Walk this way and be a good royal.

Isaac disappears in the distance, and thunder rumbles in the sky.

I head into the school and meet the musicians.

"Oh, hey, I know this guy!" The bass player picks up a drumstick and points it at me. She's a tall girl with a long black ponytail, and she wears a denim jacket filled with buttons. "This is Isaac's friend! Jennifer, you didn't tell us he was gonna be our singer!"

"I know, we're so lucky, right?" Jennifer

waves at me from the stage and gestures to the pizza. "All of this is super last minute, so we just have to roll with the thunder. Y'all are gonna be great!"

"I'm, like, star struck," the bassist says. "I'm Miranda, Isaac's friend. Wild how we're gonna be performing together, right? Is he here with you?"

I shake my head. Just hearing his name makes my jaw clench. But I won't say anything about our fight—it's not their business. "It's nice to meet you," I say. "I look forward to sharing our music."

Miranda fans herself with her hand. "God, you're so *cute*!"

Warmth floods my face, and I don't know what to say.

"Yeah, he is!" A second musician stands from behind a keyboard. "Taylor Summers. Welcome to our makeshift band."

The drummer simply nods at me and takes his drumstick from Miranda. He wears a funny hat, a dark pair of sunglasses, and a black leather jacket. He doesn't say a word all night, but the others call him Rob.

Making music with strangers is fulfilling. We

share a language for the next couple of hours. Even though we come from different worlds and kingdoms, we draw from the same pain, the same joy, and the same hope. Our hearts blend and create a melody, and it's not perfect, but it's real. And every time we share a song, the rhythm helps me feel like I understand them all—even the silent drummer.

I realize I'm not just drawing emotions from Veron anymore; I'm drawing from Belhaven. The music isn't just made of longing to break a curse, of Samuel and Aurora and my parents, or of feeling alone. It's also made of autumn wind, of sharing heartbreak with a friend, and of the joys of movies and ice cream.

It's made of Isaac. And something about him has amplified my voice today.

I don't want us to be mad at each other. This can't be the way we spend our final hours in Belhaven together. I want to leave with joy. I want to leave him with light.

Jennifer looks pleased at the end of rehearsal, and Miranda is jumping around with her bass, her ponytail swaying back and forth.

"Well," Miranda says. "I think we have a

pretty solid set list and a beautiful, shared sound. I can't believe this is happening, and I don't know how I'm going to sleep tonight! But now we need to talk about a shared look. Do you all have costumes already?"

"I'm gonna do a skeleton thing," Taylor says. "Trust me. Under the black lights, it's gonna be awesome."

"All right, Bones McGee! That rocks," Miranda says. "Rob?"

The drummer uses his stick to point at everything he's wearing. Hat. Glasses. Jacket.

Miranda nods her approval. "Okay, you can get away with that. Behind a drum set, at least. It rocks. How about our star?" She leans really close to me and flutters her glittering eyelashes. I catch a whiff of peppermint. "What's your costume tomorrow?"

I take a step back and pick up my guitar. "A prince."

"A prince?" Miranda wrinkles her nose. "That doesn't really rock, no offense. I saw your costume the other day, and while it's cute, you can be a prince at a Renaissance festival, on the dance floor, or in my dreams. But you're up here tomorrow, and you're center stage! Everyone's gonna see you and hear you, so you need to get up here and *own* it, my man." She pounds a fist into her palm. "You need to channel the hottest rock star you can think of. When you look good, you feel good. Not that you don't ever look good, because yeah. Just . . . sell it."

I scratch my head. "Sell it?"

Miranda tilts her head back and shuts her eyes. "I can see this isn't making sense."

Taylor jumps in. "Think of someone you wanna impress, and then become their rock star. If you do that, you'll win a ton of people over."

I look to Rob. He gives the thumbs up and stays silent.

Miranda laughs. "It's not like you have to try very hard, Jack. You could find something at a thrift shop and make it look good. But since nobody asked me . . ." She clears her throat and makes a heroic, goddess-like pose, fists on her waist. "I'm going to be the Silver Sorceress tomorrow. Because she rocks."

"Who's the Silver Sorceress?" I ask.

"Dude, you're like, from another time." Miranda giggles. "I love it. Find something cool, okay?"

"Cool," I repeat. "You got it."

Jennifer hands us each some cash. "Half of what I've promised," she says. "You get the other half tomorrow. You all can get here as early as three-thirty. We'll be setting up, and you can rehearse. Doors open at six o'clock sharp. They're gonna love you!"

Jennifer's compliments lift my spirits, but my fight with Isaac still weighs on me. I don't know how to make him happy without revealing everything and bringing Nev's wrath on me. Why can't he be more understanding? I grip my guitar case so hard my fingers turn red.

And then an idea comes to me.

Think of somebody you want to impress, and then become their rock star.

"Uh, Miranda?" I ask. "Where's the thrift shop?"

She beams. "It's called Second Chances. Two streets down by the Moo Factory. Can't miss it."

I walk straight there after rehearsal. I feel no need to rush home since Isaac is staying with a friend.

At Second Chances, I only spend about twenty minutes browsing before I find what I'm looking for, and stars and gods, when I look in the mirror, I *rock*. Miranda will be proud. In fact, I like it so much that I wear it out of the store.

As soon as I step outside the doors, something icy clamps down on the back of my neck.

Fingers.

I don't need to turn around to know it's Nev.

My hand falls to my waist, searching out my dagger. But my fingers only touch empty air, and I instantly regret putting the knife in Isaac's lockbox.

My body goes numb, the chill spreading all the way to the tips of my toes. I'm frozen to my core. I can't fight back when the Winter Queen struts in front of me, her silver gown swishing in the wind. She stops and looks me up and down.

"What a mess you're making of things," she says. "I give you credit. You've come much, much closer to breaking my curse than I ever expected. I banish you to this quiet little Earth dweller town, and you shake its foundation and make it fall in love with you. But what was that spectacle outside the school today? An argument, the day before your grand exit? You clearly must not care for the boy to leave him on such *frosty* terms. I hate to see it."

My jaw tenses and I can feel my nostrils flaring. They're the only muscles that move, even as I will my fists to strike and my legs to run. Every bone in my body wants to make Nev feel what I'm feeling right now, which is trapped and angry. How could she say I don't care for Isaac?

Does she even know what it's like to care?

Does she even have a heart underneath all that ice?

Nev pretends to wipe a tear from her eye, then draws a shaky breath. "And the worst part is, that boy is going to feel so devastated that you're leaving him like this. Without a goodbye. But you're going to get *your* wish, Jack. You've grown rather fond of the Earth dwellers. You wanted to experience their lives. Well, tomorrow is the celebration they call Halloween."

She shows all her teeth in a wicked grin.

"All Hallows Eve. For one night a year, they invite the Gray Lady into their homes and they dance with the mistress of death. They revel in fear and bask in terror. Chaos becomes their source of joy. And so, Jack, tomorrow I will give Halloween the touch of winter it's been missing. I will play the role of the Gray Lady."

My heart drops into my stomach, and I'm powerless. Nev's supposed to leave Belhaven alone! The people of the town have done nothing to her. Her conflict is with *me*. What is she planning for Halloween?

Nev lifts on her toes and spreads her arms over her head. The clouds darken to ash.

"And you will experience the meaning of fear," she says, "because you'll spend it all alone."

My muscles pulse, struggling to break free from the invisible bonds Nev has created. My jaw aches as though she's screwed it shut. I focus as hard as I can, willing some part of my body to move.

With an effort that leaves me winded, my jaw comes unhinged. "Nev, no!" I croak, my cheeks numb. "I still have one more day!"

Nev snaps her fingers and my jaws snap shut again, my teeth crashing together. She leans forward, her breath chilly against my ear. "You've given too many hints, darling. I cannot allow you to meddle any further. It's time we tightened the stakes, Jack."

She whispers three more words to me, each crackling with venom:

"*Sleep*, my son . . .."

FRIDAY, OCTOBER 31

THE CURSE OF THE GRAY LADY

NINETEEN

ISAAC

If Jack weren't already cursed, I would curse him with every breath in my lungs right now.

I seem to be on a roller coaster this week, and even though it scrambles my brain and makes me sick like some of my favorites, this isn't the fun kind.

Sunday and Monday, I was plunging toward rock bottom. I was furious with Seth, and with myself for letting him get to me. I was convinced I was going crazy or being stalked by some deranged illusionist. By Tuesday night, I was trekking up one of those comfortable hills, enjoying the breeze and the promise of what was to come. In a time when nothing makes sense and everything bites, Jack became a rare breath of joy. Not only that—his existence brought meaning. Suddenly my parents started wanting to go out to movies again. Life wasn't all about the future anymore. Wednesday was the day when I felt we could finally start enjoying moments again—songs and desserts and everyday car rides . . . and even family selfies.

Yesterday, I was truly at the top of the hill, even if Seth put a little corkscrew in my day. I finally knew I could handle those because Jack had my back. And maybe that's my problem. When I start to really trust someone like that, I want to know they'll stick around forever. It's why I was okay spending a few lunches apart from Armand or from Sun. We don't talk about college much but have a shared understanding that we're not getting rid of each other, no matter where we go in a few years. We've already decided we'll eventually become the old geezers who complain to each other at bingo nights. What's one or two lunches when we have forever?

But Jack isn't forever, so I spent all last night plummeting down the hill at a vertical drop.

I guess I knew all this on some level. But I thought even if Jack wasn't forever, we'd at least have high school. Even freshman year would've been cool. At least that's what I've been telling myself. The truth is, I wish he didn't even have to go home. I know that's selfish, and I really do want what's best for him—even if I was so harsh with him yesterday. I didn't mean to call him an embarrassment.

It's just that if he leaves, then that means no friendship is promised forever. Even with Sun and Armand.

The difference is that Sun and Armand didn't tell me they have to either leave Belhaven or die.

And if they ever found themselves in Jack's situation, I'd like to believe they'd trust me enough to let me help them.

With Jack, though, all he's proven is that his curse is more powerful than our friendship.

So, for Friday, Halloween, I spend the school day coasting on a flat track. The halls crackle with all kinds of energy I can't match. I'm basically on autopilot. It's a good thing nobody treats Halloween like a real school day. Everyone's all decked out in a full assortment of costumes, and it feels like I'm the only one who didn't dress up. During the passing periods, teachers pop out of their classrooms and toss chocolates and snacks around while a bunch of Halloween music plays over the speakers. The healthy treats end up all over the floor, of course. This creates some problems when the science department does their *Thriller* flash mob in the hall. But I will give props to Mrs. McKelvey, the last zombie standing.

Even if someone stripped away all the streamers, fake cobwebs, and bloody handprints, there would still be a different vibe in the air today. The people who don't care about the candy or the costumes? They crowd around the doors and take pictures of the windows, as if none of them have ever seen our boring school grounds before.

The thing is, none of us have ever seen weather quite like this. Farmer Elaine and her crystal ball—or the forecasters on the news— were right. There's a big storm on the way.

Black clouds circle Belhaven like overgrown lazy bats, threatening to burst at any moment.

Dry leaves gather on the ground and dance in swirls, then fly away. All the barren tree branches bend in the same direction and whistle in the wind. For most of the day, speculation looms that the principal is about to cancel the Fall Ball.

I listen to the rumors with casual disinterest.

Since the big argument with Jack last night, I'm not so sure I'm excited to go anymore. This is just another roller coaster he put me on. I was perfectly happy with the idea of staying home tonight. If it hadn't been for Jack, I wouldn't have even had a reason to wander into the costume shop yesterday. Now I've spent money on some cheap pirate outfit I can't return. Plus, there's the fact that Sun cut things off with Seth and made everything weird. Part of me crosses my fingers that she'll back out and I can just go donate my costume to Second Chances. Miranda will be furious if I don't go see her perform, but whose wrath have I not incurred this week?

As if Miranda can hear my thoughts, she finds me in one of the passing periods, a pair of bright red sunglasses nesting on top of her head. She takes me by both shoulders and leans in until our noses are almost touching. Her eyes gleam with typical Miranda joy.

"Your new friend is the *best human*. I'm obsessed with him."

I lean back and wrinkle my brows. "Miranda, how much Halloween candy have you had today?"

"All of it. I've had *all* the candy, and I don't care." Miranda lets go and does a full turn on the ball of one foot. "But if Principal Galvin cancels the Fall Ball and ruins my big break, I will unleash the fury of the stars and gods tonight. Will you join me?"

I dodge a flying apple that comes in from the side. "Did you just say *stars and gods*?"

Miranda's shoulders sink and she bites her lip. "You're right, it doesn't sound cool when I say it, huh?"

The school speakers buzz with static, and Principal Galvin clears her throat. "Dragons!" she says. "Thank your stars and gods today. A decision has been made. Rain or shine, the Fall Ball goes on. Happy Halloween, folks!"

Thunderous cheers and jeers ring out in the hall and candy flies everywhere.

Miranda screams, then pulls me into a full-bodied embrace. A few seconds later, Sun and Armand are also in my field of view, dancing to *Thriller*.

Apparently, nobody's backing down. They're just gathering momentum. We're all going.

"I'll see you in the crowd!" Miranda slides her sunglasses down over her eyes, makes a pair of finger guns at me, and moonwalks away.

Half-heartedly, I do the finger guns back. "Yeah. See ya there."

The temperature dips about ten degrees while I walk home, and I rub my elbows through my flannel. The pirate costume probably won't keep me warm tonight. Belhaven doesn't get this chilly until late December, and even then, it almost never storms in this town.

While I walk, I mentally rehearse hypothetical conversations with Jack. He hasn't messaged me all day, so I'm betting he's still mad. He doesn't strike me as the aggressive, confrontational type, though. My prediction—I'll walk into my bedroom, and he'll be strumming his guitar, surfing the web, or generally giving me the cold shoulder. In that case, I'll just give him more of the same. I'll play chicken all day with him until he's the first to apologize.

And in that spirit of pettiness, I prepare for scenario two, where I walk in, and Jack will be brooding. Staring at all the dark clouds and stewing in his guilt.

In that case, then *maybe* I'll be the first to apologize.

So, I'm completely caught off guard when I walk into my bedroom and confront an entirely different scenario . . . .. Jack's not even here.

I look around the house. Check under the bed. Make sure the bathroom's empty.

No boy. No pumpkin.

I stare into my empty room and think.

Did Jack even come home last night? I did tell him not to bother coming back. And it just now hits me that that was the stupidest thing I ever could've said to him, because where else would he have gone? Where could he have slept in peace without being seen in his *other* form?

Farmer Elaine's, maybe? Back to the

pumpkin patch where he can *kind of* barely blend in?

No. Jack may not know much about our culture, but by now he must understand that he'd be found there. He'd be taken home and . . . carved.

My skin goes cold. What if that's what happened? What if Jack fell asleep in some parking lot or a public place, did his transformation act, and then somebody got him?

I almost text Mom and Dad to ask if Jack ever came home. They probably assumed he was coming to Armand's house with me last night, so they wouldn't have been suspicious if they didn't see him.

I type out a message to my parents, then hesitate. Maybe it's not time to panic quite yet. If I send this message, they'll leave work and scour the town. Then I'll have to find a way to explain why Jack and I were arguing last night, along with what might've happened to him. Honestly, I think that conversation *may* even be harder than coming out was.

There's also a best-case scenario—Jack's still around, he's fine, and now he's at rehearsal, getting ready for the Fall Ball. After all, the guitar's not here.

Yes. This is what I choose to believe.

Until my phone lights up with a text from Miranda.

> **Hey you! We were wondering if Jack is on his way? We're about to start rehearsal and we haven't seen him.**

Now I know instinctively that something's wrong. Jack was over-the-moon thrilled about the chance to play for a crowd tonight. This was his chance to make some magic for Belhaven.

But his mood was a little different when I was walking him to rehearsal yesterday. He seemed distracted and sad, and then he dropped his bomb on me about how he has to die or go home soon.

I have one final idea, and I open my closet. Piece by piece, I crack the case.

The first clue is that all of Jack's princely garb is gone. The boots, gloves, tunic, and all. I grasp at a glimmer of hope that maybe he's on his way to rehearsal. He wouldn't wear that outfit anywhere else but to the Fall Ball now—not when he finds jeans and T-shirts so comfortable and when he told me he's feeling un-princely lately.

I reach up into the closet and pull out my lockbox.

Jack's dagger is gone—the special knife that's supposed to protect him from curses. And I know he wouldn't take it to school.

A weight drops in my stomach.

Jack's been home. I'm not sure if it was today or last night, but if he came back for the dagger and his suit, that means he's made a plan. The missing suit should mean he's on his way to the Fall Ball, but the missing dagger means he's *not* on his way to the Fall Ball.

He's removed every trace of himself from my life.

Jack left Belhaven just like he warned.

He's gone.

TWENTY

ISAAC

Miranda has graduated from texts to phone calls.

I sit in my dark closet letting my phone go to voicemail. I don't have the energy to listen, but I don't need to. The clock says it all.

The doors to the Fall Ball open in twenty minutes, and everyone's expecting Jack to be there. They're about to be sorely disappointed.

Jennifer's freaking, Miranda texts. **AND SO AM I. She doesn't have a Plan-C, except for the stupid music on her phone and she already paid us half! What the heck, man? Answer your phone.**

And what am I supposed to say? That Jack's on his way? That he ditched town and left me without a goodbye?

He ditched town and left me without a goodbye.

That's the easiest way to put it. That's what I have to tell my friends and my parents. When I think about this, my roller coaster of a week flies off the rails and crashes to the ground.

Mom will be compassionate and show me lots of love, but the next time I want to help a friend in need or take someone in, she won't trust them.

Dad will never trust another human again. Not when he gave away his prized guitar to someone who left three days later.

My friends will probably never trust *me* again. They expect me to be Jack's spokesman. His manager, or whatever. Whatever happens tonight is a reflection of me. If my friend no-shows at the first ever Fall Ball, that's on me. I might as well never come back to school.

And me? I'm just never gonna trust again. Period.

I shut off my phone and fling it against the wall. I'm lucky the screen stays intact.

Nobody gets an explanation tonight. I'm *not* Jack's spokesman. I'm not his anything.

If I were even his friend, he wouldn't have left things the way we left them last night. He would've said goodbye.

Fuming, I tilt my head back. It thumps against the wall of my closet, and then something unfamiliar topples into my lap. I look down to find a messy stack of notebook paper, fringes curling at the edge, and all the pieces held together by one staple.

This is not my work. All of this is perforated paper, and when I tear something out of a notebook, I'm way too finicky about getting all the fringes off.

I flick the light switch on, and I'm floored by the crisp, meticulous handwriting—my handwriting kind of looks like a serial killer's. Right now, I'm staring at the penmanship of an angel.

And I begin to read:

Hello.

This is my freewriting. We're supposed to say whatever's on our heart right now. Recently, I made a friend who told me his heart was broken, and Samuel tells me that stories are good for broken hearts. Isaac's teacher says this freewriting is just for me. But if you ever find this and your heart is still broken, then this is for you, too.

I'd like to tell you a story to remember me by.

My heart catches in my throat. Maybe Jack *did* find a way to say goodbye.

Growing up, I knew of two kingdoms— Veron, the Summer Kingdom, and Invera, the Winter Kingdom. They aren't divided by ocean, valley, or wall— just a thin, invisible curtain of magic where the snow ends and the sun begins. Samuel used to show me maps of the ages, and in the earliest times, long before my great-great-grandparents were even ideas, there were four realms. Invera absorbed the others, consuming relentlessly until it covered most of the map. Now, Veron has one corner of the land and some of the sea. It's been like this for generations.

The story goes on, and it's straight out of a fairytale.

I learn about the wisdom of Jack's mentor, Samuel.

I learn about the schemes of Nev, the Winter Queen, and a chill goes down my spine.

I learn about the arranged marriage between Jack and Princess Aurora, and for the first time, I learn what happened at the wedding.

Aurora didn't run away.

Jack did.

I'm reminded of my brief relationship with Sun, how she filled such an important space in my heart, but there was a tiny little void that she *couldn't* fill—not for any fault of her own, but because we weren't hardwired to spark the way other couples do. Only someone like Seth could complete the puzzle for me.

I always thought puzzles only had one solution, and that's why I had so much trouble getting over Seth. But now I get it. Some puzzles have *two* solutions, or more. Seth's hardwired to spark with someone like me *and* someone like Sun, and both solutions can be true.

And that's also why Aurora and Jack tried to protect each other at their wedding. Even though they knew they weren't destined for love, they could still show up for one another. In fact, they almost sacrificed themselves.

That's how I got Jack.

I read on.

As a tingle spread down my body, I spent the last of my energy trying to push Aurora out of Nev's path. I had no idea what was coming—only that it wouldn't be good. Perhaps all my training with Samuel had prepared me. After all, we'd brainstormed a thousand curses.

Vinecrawler?

Dragon?

Loss of all my senses?

No. Reality is always stranger.

I suppose the Winter Queen turned me into a pumpkin.

I should tell you that that's not all. Nev has since tightened her curse, and I will endanger the lives of my new friends if I reveal too much to them.

I should also tell you that this is my first time being cursed, and so far, the experience isn't living up to my expectations. It's supposed to be a punishment, yet I'm enjoying it. I can't help but feel that the true curse is yet to come.

You see, growing up, I knew of two kingdoms, and I'm supposed to bring them together. This is the duty of a prince, and this is what I must do. To Veron, I shall return, and I shall protect the hearts of my people from the eternal winter.

But if you're reading this, you should know that I've left half of my heart in a third kingdom.

I don't think I know what true love is, but

I do love this kingdom called Belhaven.

I love its sorcery. The internet has taught me more than wizards ever could.

I love its food. I thought maybe I'd broken the curse when I first tried pizza.

I love its music. There are new melodies that have been written into my bones.

Above all, I'm reminded of a time when Samuel said that love was a meeting of the stars, like sunlight filling you from your head to toe. I think that maybe for the first time, I've met another star. Except in all the stories, the two stars are a prince and a princess, so I can't be sure this feeling is real. The star I've found isn't a princess. It's someone more like me.

I do know that being cursed feels like the greatest gift I've ever been given. I'll spend the rest of my life trying to bring these three kingdoms together. Then all the stars can be visible.

May the gods smile on you.

When I finish reading, I can barely breathe. Stars and gods.

Jack wrote all of this in English yesterday. And he was . . . he was starting to have feelings for—

Before I can finish my thoughts, a pebble hits my bedroom window.

Great. Now that my phone's off, student council and my friends are sending each other to my house.

A second pebble strikes.

I spring to my feet and rush to open my window. "Are you gonna pay if you break my window? Get out of here!"

Wait a second.

The person in my driveway is the last guy I expected to see. Seth waves at me, dropping the tiny rocks he's holding. A sheet of pale white makeup coats his face, and he spits a set of plastic vampire teeth into his hand. "Isaac! Can you come down?"

I roll my eyes. Could the dude be any more cliché? "Get out of here, man. I'm not going to the Fall Ball."

"Wait!" I have the window halfway down when another pebble strikes.

"I'm not kidding," I say. "If you break the window I swear—"

"Just come down? Please? I need one minute of your time. That's it." He gives me that stupid puppy dog look I've come to hate so much. "One minute, or I break your window."

My blood boils. I owe him nothing. Especially if he's coming over just to bounce back after his breakup with Sun.

He curls back his arm, aiming the rock.

"I hate you so much," I say. "Put the rock down. I'll be there in a sec."

I shuffle downstairs.

When I open the front door, Seth looks frantic. For a second, I think he's covered in sweat, but then I realize his makeup is full of glitter. "I have to say something," he says. "I know you probably don't want to hear it, but it's really important."

I glance at my watch. "You have one minute."

Seth takes a deep breath, preparing for his big spiel, and then lets it all out in one sentence. "Isaac, I'm really sorry about everything."

Four seconds. Keeping my eyes on my watch,

I ask, "Is that it?"

"That's it," Seth says. "That's the thing. I'm done. For whatever it's worth, relationship or no relationship, Sun or no Sun, I miss you. I miss our friendship, and I'm really sorry that I've hurt you, and I want us to be cool again. You just had to know that."

My gaze falls away from my watch and goes to my feet. This is one of those times when I can't meet his eyes directly, because that's where I always seemed to start drowning before.

Aw, whatever. I'm a stronger guy now. I look him square in the eyes, and I realize he's wearing cheap gold contact lenses.

"Wait . . ... Are you supposed to be Edward Cullen?"

Seth runs a hand through his hair. "So you noticed."

I wave a hand over my face. "The sparkles are overkill." I sigh. "And I'm sorry, too. I was really childish about all this. And you know what? I kind of did the same thing to Sun a long time ago. We moved on. We're still best friends. We're better for it now. Maybe you and I can be, too."

Seth clutches his chest, then extends his hand. "So, we're bros now?"

"No. Better." I shake his hand and we lock it in. "*Friends*. If that's cool with you."

"Friends," Seth repeats. "I like that. A lot, actually. And since we're friends, I have something in my car that I really want you to see."

I narrow my eyes, thinking of all the Halloween pranks this could lead to. Maybe all of this is a mistake. My guard flies up.

Seth notices. "Just please come see what's in my car? If it's a prank, you have *all* the blackmail on me. Just let me tell you what happened. I *really* wasn't planning to go to the Fall Ball today. I was so mad at everything with Sun, and things were gonna be awkward, and Phil vs. the Specters cancelled. I didn't want to go."

I cross my arms. "Let me guess. Miranda bullied you?"

"Seriously, she always gets her way." Seth claws at his hair. "We went back and forth over it all day, and she's especially mean right now because I guess their singer hasn't shown up yet. But anyway, I caved about an hour ago. I didn't even have a costume ready to go, so she sent me to that little thrift shop. You know, Second Chances?"

"I know the place," I say. "What does that have to do with anything?"

Seth holds up a hand as if to say, *I'm getting to it.* "Second Chances. It got me thinking about how I really want to make things up to you, and to Sun, and to everyone. I don't know if you believe in fate or whatever. But I went into Second Chances and I scraped together this ridiculous Twilight costume. And I *know* Jacob's hotter, but that's beside the point. The point is that on my way out, it was so crazy. You won't believe what I stole from the window display."

My eyes widen. "What did you do, Seth? Shoplifting? Really? How were you gonna judge me for stealing a 'prop' from the corn maze last Sunday?"

"That's what's wild." Seth runs to his car and unlocks the passenger door. "Look. Open the door."

To shut him up, I do what I'm told.

And I just about drop when I see the blue pumpkin in the passenger seat.

TWENTY-ONE

ISAAC

Time accelerates, and I'm riding my roller coaster again.

I throw my arms around the pumpkin. From now on, I'm not letting it go. Nev can pry it from my cold dead hands if she wants it back. "Jack!"

Seth scratches his head and gives me the side-eye.

I turn around and hug him, too. "Thank you, Seth!"

He gives me two slaps on the back and says, "Um. Isaac I think you might be confused right now. That is a pumpkin."

My mind races. "Yes! Yes, it is. It's my pumpkin and it's the best one ever and—oh man, this pumpkin is super late for the Fall Ball!"

Seth checks the time on his phone. "Calm down, Cinderella. Fall Ball's just starting. Do you mean to tell me you're still coming? Because now everyone's blowing up my phone and they can't get a hold of you and I don't really know what to tell anyone. If you ride with me, we can be there in five."

"Yes, yes, I'm going! Can I trust you to watch this pumpkin for one minute while I get shoes on?"

"I'm timing you." Seth readies his keys and pops his plastic teeth into his mouth. I strain my hearing to make out the words. "And trust? After all the trouble I went through to bring it back to you?"

"Don't put any more holes in it!" I call from the door.

I throw on my shoes, grab my phone, and I'm out of the house in a flash.

Pirate Isaac won't be appearing at the Fall Ball tonight, but that's okay.

The people want Jack, and I'm going to get him there.

I bounce in Seth's car seat all the way to the

school, clinging onto the pumpkin like it's going to melt away tomorrow. For all I know, it could. I inspect it for any new bruises, cuts, holes, or marks that would hurt Jack in his human form. It's a little scuffed, like it's been rolled around on a sidewalk, but I think he'll be okay.

I just hope he still has time and that this isn't his "forever form."

Seth is grinning at me, and I know he's silently judging. "Do I even want to know what's up with that thing? I mean, I thought you loved it on Sunday, but now?"

Love.

The words I found today are on loop. Jack's whole tale.

"It's a long story, Seth." I adjust my seatbelt. "We do not have time for it. But I have a question of my own—how did this end up at Second Chances?"

Seth shrugs. "That's what I asked the lady today. She said she's always had it and that she's been putting it in the Halloween window display for years. I told her she was lying and that my friend found it at Farmer Elaine's on Sunday. I even showed her Elaine's WowFeed! And she just kept insisting it belonged to her. She was kind of weird. Her exact words were, '*He belongs to my kingdom.*' Yeah, whatever, lady. I crawled up in the display, snagged the pumpkin, and bolted when she wasn't looking."

Seth's story puts a pit in my stomach, but I'm grateful for him. "Thank you," I say as the school comes into view. "Truly."

"Of course. I know how much that thing means to you. Or maybe I don't. I'm not gonna try to understand it anymore." He parks the car. "I just wanna go dance, have fun with my friends, and be a happy vampire this Halloween."

"Jacob's still hotter." I mash the button on my seatbelt. "Come on, let's hurry inside!"

Seth clutches his chest like he's been wounded, and I sprint to the gym doors with a blue pumpkin in my arms.

To my horror, people trickle out of the gym in a thin but steady stream. A few people go inside, but the ratio is clear—there are definitely more people leaving than entering.

"Seriously, no live music?" people mutter. "That's like the number one thing we were promised."

"First ever Fall Ball? More like *Fail* Ball."

"Let's hit the haunted house at the fire department."

And suddenly, I'm acting like a fool. "Go back inside! Go back inside! The singer's here."

I get some serious side-eye, but I seem just crazy enough that people can't wait to watch the drama unfold. Belhaven's first Fall Ball needs a good story for people to gossip about tomorrow.

Seth follows me into the gym doors, and I rush past the table at the entrance. "Wait!" the ghost at the table calls. "Where's your donation of money or food or blood?"

"I'm with the band!" I call.

If this works out, I'll give the student countsil every dollar in my wallet later. For now, I keep moving, and I don't dare look over my shoulder. If I trip with this pumpkin in my hands and it breaks on the ground . . .? Oof.

Miranda stands up on the stage in a ritzy red costume with two other musicians I don't know very well. She stares daggers at me when we lock eyes. She jumps off the stage, and we make a beeline for each other.

"Seriously, Isaac?" She hasn't lost any of her energy from earlier in the day—she's just dialed it from hype to anger. "This is the most humiliating night of my life. I've been trying to get a hold of you for *three hours,* and now you show up ten minutes late to the Fall Ball with that weird pumpkin in your hands? Where's Jack?"

I push past her. "Get back on stage, Miranda."

"What? Did you even hear me? Where's—"

"He's right here. Get back up there."

"Isaac." Miranda grits her teeth. "People are *stariiing.*"

And maybe they are. I'll probably even end up all over WowFeed soon, but I don't care. I have tunnel vision for the stage. I don't stop moving until I reach it.

I set the pumpkin down behind the front mic. Center stage. Spotlight burning.

Then I lean in.

"Jack," I whisper. "If you can hear me, it's time to wake up. It's time for your big debut."

Somebody's hand warms my shoulder, and Sun's voice speaks into my ear. "Isaac," she says. "Maybe we should go get some air."

"Wait for it," I say.

I believe in this. I have to.

Miranda picks up her bass. The keyboardist and the drummer are completely still, and so is the pumpkin.

I nod at Miranda. "Start playing something." I step back from the stage. "Just trust me."

The band members look at each other and exchange some sort of non-verbal cue.

The drummer clicks his sticks.

Miranda plucks a string.

The keyboardist plays a chord.

And after a flash of light, Jack emerges from the pumpkin, guitar and all.

A startled *oh!* rolls through the gym, and the crowd explodes with thunderous applause.

Jack doesn't miss a beat, literally. He jumps right into the music with Miranda and the band, strumming and crooning and dancing like he'll never dance again.

"Wow," I breathe.

He's not in his royal garb like he planned. Instead, he wears a shimmering jacket, matching pants, and a velvet vest. I think he's trying to be Chris D'Agosto.

But I have a new favorite musician now.

I see the guy on stage for everything he is, and Jack is a lot of things. He's all at once a prince and a town boy. A singer and a storyteller. A boy under a curse and a boy with a great gift. A guy with a foot in two kingdoms, and tonight, he shows off his whole world.

Like Frankenstein's monster rising from his table, the sad gymnasium sizzles to life. The disco ball begins to turn. Colored lights swirl, painting the band in electric hues. The beat throbs under the hardwood floor and people dance. They sway and rock and shine the flashlight on their phones.

And me? I think I'm hypnotized by the singer.

Jennifer rushes up to me, jumping up and down. "Isaac! How in the world did you pull that off? The pumpkin trick? Everyone's trying to figure it out, and we're all like, Phil vs. the Who? This is incredible!"

Seth has one eyebrow raised. "You could've told me that was gonna happen."

"Or me," Armand says. "All that time you were at my house last night and no preview?"

Sun hands me a cup of punch. "I'm glad

you came." She raises her own cup. "Cheers."

We crash plastic cups.

She leans in. "Okay, seriously, though. How'd you do that?"

I look to the stage, and Jack winks at me.

"It's magic," I say.

"Well, whatever it is . . .?" Jennifer does the *mind blown* gesture, sound effects and everything. "It's a dream."

I agree. But the boy on stage is still cursed and the storm continues to build outside.

I can't help but feel like there's still time for the dream to end and for Halloween to go horribly wrong.

TWENTY-TWO

JACK

So, this is Halloween.

In defiance of Nev, I'm here. And every word she told me was wrong.

This crowd doesn't dance with the Gray Lady. They dance with *me*, every one of them, and my song is a melody of life and joy.

On the Fall Ball stage, I embrace the spirit of Belhaven and its beautiful energy, letting it spread through every note I play.

Nev thought she was going to ruin Halloween?

I *am* Halloween.

She wanted to curse Belhaven with paralyzing fear?

I want her to see their joy.

I find Isaac in the crowd, and for a moment, I think our hearts connect. He smiles again. This lifts me up and powers my music, because maybe he does still care. Even though we fought last night, he still found me and woke me up. He gave me one more cursed night in Belhaven, and this curse is a gift.

Because up here, playing this song, I feel like *me*. I feel real. And I look at Isaac and see the real him, the way I want to remember him. He looks happy. He's surrounded by his friends—even the one I don't like, Seth the enzyme. But Isaac's heart doesn't look so broken anymore.

It looks the way mine feels. Full.

I have to leave soon.

I can't leave without saying goodbye, even if I've written my story down. There's a chance Isaac may never find it, and he deserves a proper farewell. I just don't know how to say goodbye any other way.

So instead of saying it, I wrap it in music.

I don't put words to it because I can't find them. I just let the strings speak through me.

With my melody, I try to tell Isaac that I have to go soon, but that I'm going to be okay.

And that I think that maybe he will, too. And that if I can find a way to visit or bring our kingdoms together, I'll do it the first chance I get. Promise.

Applause rings through the crowd, but all I see is Isaac.

He smiles through a layer of tears and nods his understanding.

All I have to do now is say the magic words. I'm ready for them.

I take a deep breath. I close my eyes.

And the power fizzles out in the school, plunging the Fall Ball into darkness.

The doors open, and time *slows* . . ..

Everything goes ice cold.

TWENTY-THREE

JACK

Excited murmurs spread through the gym.

Most folks are startled by the power outage. They stumble in the dark and try to ground their position. But with so many bodies in one space, a number of them fall and tumble over each other's feet.

The optimistic people in the crowd snicker and whisper that this is all a Halloween prank. They wish to believe one of their own had cut off the power, and I wish to tell them they're correct.

Slowly, everyone looks to the doors. Cold wind rushes into the building, blowing in white bits of fuzz that evaporate as soon as they land on a warm body. I remember a time when I longed for this. So many days I would sit in front of the invisible curtain that separated Veron and Invera, putting my fingers as close to the frost as possible without crossing the boundary. Tonight, the boundary has come to me.

"Whoa," Taylor the keyboardist says. "It's snowing."

My eyes adjust to the dark and I scan the crowd for Isaac, who's already pushing his way to the stage with his friends.

I jump down and meet him in front of the stage. Before I can say a word, he throws his arms around me in a tight hug. "Jack, you're still here. I'm sorry about everything I said yesterday, and I care so, so much about you. You're not weird, you're awesome. The only reason I was so mad is because I wasn't ready for you to leave. But whatever happens—"

"Isaac." I gently pull away from his hug and rest my hands on his shoulders, my mind in full survival mode. Nev is coming, and I must be ready to protect Belhaven. All my training with Samuel kicks in. "There's no time for this. I know. I wasn't ready to leave you, either. But right now, you're in danger, and it's my fault. I need my dagger. Do you have it with you? Or can you leave the school and get it for me?"

Isaac shakes his head, his eyes widening. "No. I thought maybe you had it. I looked in the lockbox today and I thought you left because your knife wasn't there anymore." He lifts my hand off his shoulder and gives my palm a squeeze. "Jack, if it's the Winter Queen, I can help you fight her. I don't know how, but if defeating Nev can help you break the curse, I'll do anything. Even if that means you have to go home. I'll protect you."

The Winter Queen. Nev. I've been very careful not to say these names around Isaac before, and now he's called her by name.

He's read everything I wrote down. My story. My thoughts and feelings.

I left it all for Isaac yesterday before rehearsal, just in case, but I didn't want him to find it until I left Belhaven. Yet there's something liberating about his knowledge, like he's opened a trap I didn't know I was caught in.

I squeeze his hand. This is the hand that

cleaned my blood when we were strangers, and since then, Isaac has shown me an entire world. After all we've shared, this will be the last time I see him, so I allow myself five seconds to memorize the warmth, pulse, and texture of his fingertips.

"You need to go home, too," I whisper. "To your family. It's not safe for you to stay here."

Isaac shakes his head. "I'm not turning my back on you again."

I turn to Isaac's friends. Armand. Sun. Seth. "Will all of you please take Isaac and go? In fact, get everyone you can out of here. Go anywhere. Lock up. Protect yourselves."

Seth rubs his forehead, smearing his shiny vampire makeup. "I just saw a pumpkin turn into a dude, and I don't know what life is anymore. Is something bad coming? Like, was there really a dragon in Belhaven all along?"

"Worse," I say simply.

That seems to be enough for Seth. "Let's get out of here."

Much of the crowd makes its way for the door. I try to ignore Isaac's protests as his friends pull him away from me. I want to remember him happy.

But he's going to be okay. He has good, loyal friends . . . even the enzyme.

Miranda huffs, and I turn to find the rest of the band still on stage with their instruments.

"Where is everyone going?" Miranda yells into the crowd. "Fall Ball isn't over! Get away from the snow. It's not that exciting. You'll see it again in December."

"Miranda," I say, "you should go, too."

"No. We still have twenty minutes until midnight, and I want to keep playing. I told Isaac earlier that if anything cancelled this show, they would feel the wrath of the stars and gods. Well, now I'll do you one better." She raises her arms over her head and yells at the ceiling, "I am the Silver Sorceress, and in the name of all that is nerdy, I demand that somebody turn the stupid power back on!"

A gasp sweeps through the crowd when the lights come back on stage.

I squint through the blinding shade of red and wrinkle my brows at Miranda. "Are you a sorceress?"

She looks startled by her own power, staring at her magic hands. "Um. Sure. I guess I am."

Another spotlight comes on and points to

the door.

A woman in white and silver saunters in, basking in the glow of the light, and everything goes quiet.

No.

My heart turns to steel.

At least Isaac and his friends are nowhere to be seen. Perhaps they made it out on time.

And all eyes are on Nev, the Winter Queen.

The people stare, presumably wondering if she's a part of the show, and they wait for her to speak as she studies the crowd.

When she begins, her voice fills the room.

"Hello, hello." The spotlight follows her into the crowd, even though nobody operates the machine. "Please allow me to introduce myself. I am your fairy godmother for the evening, and I'm here to grant all your Halloween wishes."

Nobody says a word, and I can feel the room itself holding its breath. Nev sure knows how to control a crowd.

The Winter Queen plucks an orange streamer off the wall and spins on her toes, letting the streamer coil around herself like a snake. A layer of frost blooms on the paper, tracing the ridges. "Tonight, you have been promised a frightfully good time and a healthy dose of bone-chilling entertainment. Instead, you got a handsome guitar player who was late to his own show. And I think that's so *borrring*." She pretends to shiver on the last word. "Don't you all?"

The silence holds, but Miranda doesn't buy into the trance. She leans over and hisses into my ear, "So what, she has a bunch of special effects. Big deal. Jack, get back up here. We're gonna keep playing."

Nev continues, "Would it help to know that all along, you've been living in a dark fairytale? Hmm? What if I told you that your rock star is also a prince who ruined his own wedding?" As evidence, she produces my suit from thin air, holds it up for everyone to see, and then tosses it to the ground. "What if I told you I gave him a week to do something so simple, and if he'd only upheld his end of the bargain, he could have gone home and saved Belhaven from the destruction you're about to see?"

Miranda swats me on the shoulder. "Dude, who cares what she says about you? Come on. Don't let her ruin your show."

"And so." Nev stands in the center of the room and pauses. My blood flushes cold when she snaps her fingers and my dagger appears in her hands. "I invite you to witness the ending of this dark fairytale. If someone gets hurt, I invite you to ask yourself who the *real* monster is. Every fairytale has one, and I assure you that tonight, it isn't me. If you're faint of heart, you may leave."

I don't know what to do. Nev has my dagger, possibly the one thing that can harm her. I'm good in combat, but Nev can paralyze me with the tap of her finger. I can't touch her.

All I have is music, the single strand of sorcery that woke me today. Isaac's father says this is my magic, but I wonder if the people in Belhaven overuse this word. Music can join hearts together and move souls, but it can't defeat the Winter Queen.

But Miranda has a power that turned the lights on. She has the music in every bone in her body.

Maybe she's onto something.

I ready Danny's guitar.

"Hey, lady!" Miranda yells. "You interrupted

our show! Get with the music or get lost!"

Before Nev can respond, the silent drummer thrusts his sticks over his head and clicks them together. He startles me when he screams, *"One! Two! One two three four!"*

And we blast Nev with everything we have.

The people are dancing again, and my soul is on fire with all kinds of emotions. All that magic pours out of the music. Literally. Ripples of color blast from the speakers, pelting Nev with a rainbow of light. The light touches the people of Belhaven, but they're unaffected. The ripples bounce off them in joyful patterns. The people swim in it. They glow.

But not Nev. All the light sears into her, shedding the layer of frost from her skin until she begins to drip. The waves push her across the floor, throwing her hair behind her as if she's caught in a storm. She throws her hands in front of her face to shield her eyes, the light refracting from my dagger and splashing every corner of the room.

Finally, she drops the knife.

Yes.

I lose sight of it as the crowd kicks it around.

No.

But maybe I don't need it. For the first time, I see Nev in pain, her lips curling and her cheeks weathered like the wrinkled skin of a rotting apple.

It's working! The music is my weapon, and it's strong enough!

Unfortunately, my hope is short-lived.

For a second, I think Nev is about to melt into the floor and disappear forever. But then she bares her teeth and narrows her eyes at me. She's turning her pain into anger. She finds her footing and takes one step forward, the impact of her boot sending a shockwave through the floor.

Then four long, hairy appendages burst from the back of her gown in the shape of an X.

Nev folds over. The new appendages come down, a human hand at the end of each one. They take root on the gym floor, nearly tripling her height.

Stars and gods.

We stop the music, and Miranda and the band clear the stage.

People scream at Nev's grotesque new transformation, and the Fall Ball crowd exits in a chaotic stampede.

The Winter Queen has morphed into a monstrosity that's half-human and half-vinecrawler. She towers over me, more terrifying than any creature I expected to face in the corn labyrinth. I'm powerless. I see my dagger glisten by the door, but if I make a run for it, Nev will be faster. Not even the music will save me now.

But at least Isaac is safe.

There are two minutes to midnight, and Isaac is safe.

Sweat drips from my hair and my breaths are heavy. Despite the fear that's taken root in my veins, I can only smile. No matter what Nev thinks, I've won.

"Stubborn, simple boy." Nev's voice grows deep and distorted. "So smug. I think I'll destroy you slowly, one inch at a time, and really make you feel it. You didn't want to be the prince of my kingdom, and now you shall die as the prince of nothing. I promised you the full Halloween experience. So, with your last two minutes before midnight, Jack, I think I'll make a lantern out of you."

She turns, her four new legs moving one at

a time, and goes for my dagger.

Isaac dashes into the gym, sending my heart galloping in my chest.

"No!" I cry. "Isaac, what are you doing?"

Why did he come back?

"Saving your life."

"Get out of here!"

I don't know if he doesn't hear me or if he refuses to listen, but instead of leaving, Isaac makes a dive for the knife.

But Nev gets to it first.

TWENTY-FOUR

ISAAC

In the most terrifying moment of my life, I stand in front of the monster that's been tormenting Jack. She's the most frightening sight I've ever seen—like a mutant spider. My heart slams against my ribs. I fear for my life, but most of all, I fear for Jack. And I'm *angry*. Like, blood boiling in my veins angry. All of this has been her doing. This is the woman I saw at the movie theater. She's the reason Jack was stuck in a window display at Second Chances, and she's probably even the woman Seth stole him back from. She's been watching Jack's every move, and she wants to destroy his home.

Jack stands on the stage, and all the color

drains from his face when he sees me. "Isaac," he says, his voice broken. "No."

I swallow a lump in my throat and say in my bravest, steadiest voice, "Nev. You're gonna leave Jack alone."

The Winter Queen snarls at me. "A brave, stupid Earth dweller," she says. "You've come back thinking you can save this young man. Do you know that if he cared as much as you do, his curse would be over by now? I told everyone I'm not the monster. I gave this boy options. Sure, I may have nudged him toward my *preferred* option—that he marry my daughter—but he also could have broken the spell with an act of true love. And even though you care oh-so deeply for this prince, he's still cursed. And for your information, dearest—"

She takes Jack's dagger in one of her freakish, hairy arms and raises it high. Streamers fall and a balloon bursts on the ceiling. For a second, I think she's about to bring the blade down on me, but instead, she swipes at nothing.

Where the knife falls, a rip appears in the air. She's torn a hole as easily as if the air were paper, big enough for a human to step through.

Through the hole, a forest gleams with frost.

A castle looms beyond the trees.

This is another world.

As strange and beautiful as it all is, I don't have the time to be mesmerized.

The Winter Queen smirks. "Jack's curse ends in one minute."

I shake my head. The Winter Queen is trying to make Jack seem like the bad guy—like he never cared. But I know the truth. He cares about so much that I don't see how he can fit all that love into one heart. Love of music, love of Belhaven, love of his home. How dare she try to say that he doesn't care?

She's put Jack in an impossible position. I can't keep him here, but I can keep him safe. My family promised him that.

"Take me," I say. "Whatever you're going to do with him, have me instead. Take me ransom. Just break Jack's curse and let him go free. Leave him alone, and you can have *me*."

"No!" Jack cries. "Isaac, no. Please. You don't know what you're doing."

The Winter Queen licks her lips like she's

tasted something delicious. "Oh, my! You would take Jack's fate?"

"Yes."

"You swear it?"

"Nev!" Jack falls to his knees, the guitar still around his neck. He puts his hands together. "I am begging you. Do not do this to Isaac. Don't listen to him. You will ruin me."

"Ruin you, hmm?" The Winter Queen cackles. "Oh, what a twist! Here I've been so proud to have written my finest curse, and then a simple Earth dweller has found a way to make it even more painful. You have enjoyed your curse far too much and angered me far too deeply. It just wouldn't be enough to destroy you. Perhaps if I destroy your heart, then you'll learn. And in your anguish, you'll join my Aurora and find renewed loyalty to Invera. Jack, my darling, I told you the weather can change very quickly, and now your real curse is about to begin. Isaac, you brave boy, you'll make a lovely pumpkin. Have you any final words to say with your last ten seconds?"

I smile at Jack. In one second, a week of memories flashes through my head.

It only takes one more second to say what I want to say. Six words.

For the remaining seconds, I just let the words ring. Cold pain trickles through my body, and I bear it. I stare at Jack and I take it, because he's the last thing I want to be looking at in the end.

I can't pinpoint the one moment when I knew my last words were true. I don't think it's ever as simple as the movies make it seem—where one day the cute friend starts walking in slow motion, wind in their hair, and then the other friend just *gets* it. I've been on a roller coaster all week, and I didn't blink and end up on top of the hill. There was a whole climb where Jack occasionally annoyed me. He embarrassed me. He surprised me. He scared me. He wowed me. All these things built up to something new, and now this is the way it is as I fade out of the world.

To let Jack go? To meet the Gray Lady at the top of the hill so he can go home?

I'm happy with this.

Because stars and gods . . .

I love him.

SATURDAY, NOVEMBER 1

THE DARKEST CURSE OF THEM ALL

TWENTY-FIVE

JACK

It's midnight on the eighth day, and today my real curse begins. It sears me with more fire than all the other curses I imagined with Samuel combined. A thousand possible curses, and Nev found the one I could never recover from.

My heart bursts into dust as Isaac crumples to the ground. His limbs fold into his torso, and he contorts until he's an imperfect globe, bluish-white like the core of winter.

And that's it.

Isaac's gone.

I slump to the ground, my chest wrapped in iron.

"No," I whisper. "It's not fair. You need to

undo this."

"You know that it's better this way." Nev begins to shrink, her vinecrawler appendages folding back into her body until she's just a woman again. She looks small now, but as she struts over to me, frost winds its way around her gown again. Her face returns to its usual shine.

"Do you know why my rule has lasted so long?" she asks. "It's because I never shared my heart with anyone. You give that away, and you give away your power. This boy has already made you weak. You cannot rule with a soft heart. You will recover, and you will be harder and stronger. Yes, I enjoy watching the pursuit of true love, but the folly of this is that fairytales don't exist. Love is the ultimate fairytale. Your betrothal to Aurora will be more than appropriate without love. You will still produce beautiful heirs. You will still prepare the kingdom for *my* rule, and you will do so with strength and without silly emotions clouding your head."

"But it was never supposed to be him," I choke. "He was supposed to be okay."

"I understand you are in mourning." Nev

almost sounds compassionate, her voice soft. But it's all a lie. "Don't be. Pull yourself together. Your kingdom awaits."

"No." I swallow a lump in my throat. "I'm staying with him."

"Jack," Nev says, a warning in her voice. "Be grateful that this is the extent of your punishment. If you still wish to irk me, there are more people I can take away from you. Your dear Samuel. Your beloved parents. They all live now, but everyone meets the Gray Lady one day. Has autumn taught you nothing? Father Time is the greatest thief in all the lands, dearest. No matter how well you hide, he always collects his bounty. Death is everywhere, even in the trees. So shed your leaves, Jack. Put down that foolish guitar, let the boy go, and come do your duty."

A tear carves its way down my cheek. Nev will just keep taking things from me for the rest of my life. She'll take Samuel and my parents anyway. And when she's done with me, she'll take me, too.

The best I can hope for is the chance to tell everyone what I didn't tell Isaac in person. What he told me with his final breath. Nev can take my opportunities to love, but she can never take the love out of me.

"Can I . . ." I whisper. "Can I just have one more minute to say goodbye?"

Nev clucks her tongue. "Let me put this to you one more way and see if it sticks . . .. The boy you care for is gone. That thing you see there . . .? It's just a vegetable. It has no thoughts, feelings, or heart. Do you have any memory of your time as a pumpkin, boy? No. Because every time you changed, that's all you ever were. Did your brain refuse to come back with your last transformation? It's foolish to care for a vegetable. And if this is the only way you'll let it go . . ."

She takes my dagger and moves toward the pumpkin.

The knife goes over her head, and Nev takes aim.

The words fall out of my mouth.

"I love you, too, Isaac."

And I'm back on my feet, sprinting like wind to put my body between Nev and the pumpkin.

I'm right in front of her when she brings the knife down.

The blade connects, and it's a hot iron burning everything down to my bones. White light sears my vision and screams of terror shred through my ears. The pain makes me so dizzy, I can't even tell if the screams are my own. I just know they never seem to stop.

This is all I know until I know no more.

SUNDAY, NOVEMBER 2

THE CURSE OF GOODBYE

TWENTY-SIX

ISAAC

When I wake up in the hospital, I'm convinced that the Fall Ball was a fever dream and that Jack Zuka never existed. That I conjured him in my head as some flashy rock-n-roll Halloween spirit, and he vanished with the turn of the calendar.

The pictures on my phone say otherwise, but the photos don't explain what happened at midnight. Nobody really knows. I scroll social media and people talk, but it's all speculation. Some people say this was Belhaven's best Halloween ever, and I envy the people who think it was all an elaborate trick. Others are still freaked out of their minds, and I don't blame them. But we all agree that this Halloween has been the strangest. There's a gap in my memory that I'll never fill.

That gap starts right after I said *I love you,* with the Winter Queen standing over my head.

I can trace the story back as far as Seth, Armand, Miranda, and Sun, who claim that when they found me knocked out in the gym after midnight, I *wasn't* a pumpkin and there was no Winter Queen.

There was no Jack, no hole in the air, and no knife.

There was also no snow. Everyone remembers it and says we had a full-on blizzard, but by the time my friends reached me, all that snow had melted away.

My friends carried me home, and my parents rushed me to the hospital, and I guess I was technically in a mini coma for a day. The doctors diagnosed me with a "nasty bump on the head," or at least that's been my takeaway. I wonder what the medical term would be if they knew the full story.

They say they'll keep an eye on me and that I'm well-loved, as evidenced by the chocolates, cards, and balloons on my nightstand. Mom and Dad have barely left my side. They haven't asked me very many questions, and I'm grateful because I don't have a real explanation yet. I do need them to know that Jack loved them—that he had a real reason for leaving. Maybe I'll even try out the truth and see what happens. They may not believe me, and if they do, they may not love the truth. But if there's one thing I've learned, it's that their love is unconditional.

Mrs. McKelvey's also been here and so have many of my friends. Farmer Elaine has been around, too. In fact, her card is one of my favorites. She printed out the picture of me, her, and Jack the Pumpkin, and she wrote a little message.

> You may have an admirer or two!
> A rather handsome young man came
> to see me claiming to be this pumpkin.
> Get well soon and go find this boy.

I wish I could do what she's instructed and go find Jack. But I know it's not that simple. He's gone, and that's just the way it is this time. My heart is heavy, but my heart is also full. I made that deal with the Winter Queen so he could go home. That's why nobody can find him.

It's just good to believe he's okay somewhere.

I'll think of him often. Probably every day and in bites of pizza, in sudden gusts of wind, and in beautiful song. And every time, it's going to hurt, but that's all part of the season. Autumn shows us that sometimes we have to let go of the beautiful things in our lives. Luckily, there are other seasons to bring us new joys, and I won't go through them alone. I have friends like Miranda and Sun and Seth and Armand, who insists he always knew Jack wasn't some friend I made on *Galaxy's Oceans*. Apparently Moon Mages can't specialize in Lunar Alchemy or whatever.

Whether or not she knew it, Elaine did tell me her farm would change my life, and she was absolutely right. She just didn't understand how. Jack changed a lot of things on Halloween. People will ask questions for a while, and then one day they'll just stop speaking his name. And then they'll forget about him, but for me, the dude will haunt me like a phantom.

It's almost funny. Now the people of Belhaven finally have their ghost story.

But I can't stop smiling, because some stories are like people. Some of them can't be contained in just one box. And Jack . . .? He doesn't even fit into just one world. That's how I know this isn't the end.

Because even if he's Belhaven's ghost story, for me . . . he's a different kind.

EPILOGUE

JACK

I stand in the middle of the forest where there used to be an invisible curtain between two kingdoms.

The curtain is gone now, and snow covers the land from corner to corner. But tomorrow all this snow will vanish, and Aurora will declare the first day of spring for the kingdom of Veron.

She's a wicked fine princess, and the man next to her is the best who could ever stand at her side—the best one to share her heart, the best to marry into royalty. Samuel taught me everything I knew about being a prince, so why shouldn't he become one himself?

He wraps his arm around Aurora and gives

me a look of brotherly pride.

He tells me that I've changed everything with Summer's Glow and nothing will ever be the same.

Summer's Glow.

At least, that's what we think it is.

When Nev brought her knife down on Halloween night, I don't think it touched me at all. I shielded Isaac with my body, but I was wearing a shield myself. That caused a meeting of stars.

Nev had my knife, a gift made with care by my powerful mentor. It was never meant to do harm—only to protect me from curses.

And strapped around my neck, I still had an old guitar, imbued with the love of a boy's father and devoted mother. The love of a family who offered me shelter and community.

When the knife met the guitar, the light from the collision was so intense, I could hardly bear it. But it was all worth taking, because in the end, the curse *rebounded*.

The guitar survived without a scratch.

Nev burst into a spray of snowfall, showering the gym in frost and ultimately melting away.

Isaac reverted to his human form, unconscious but unharmed. I sat next to him and played him music until his friends showed up at the gym. By then, the portal to home was closing, and I needed to see my parents. When I knew Isaac would be taken care of, I slipped away. I also whispered to him that I'd be back, and I kept Danny's guitar as proof. I would never have taken it with me if I didn't think I could bring it back someday. After all, Nev always had a way to move between worlds, and I'd find one, too.

I've been home for months now, finishing a new part of my training and celebrating the summer marriage of Samuel and Aurora. I've introduced them to the delights of autumn, and we've experienced a mild winter. The variety of seasons has brought fresh cycles of life to Veron. Knowing one season will end, we appreciate it more.

Endings are bittersweet, but we look forward to new joys.

This is what I explain to Samuel and Aurora as I prepare to leave them. Since I've been home, a wise king and queen have been visiting from a faraway land, and they've taught me to use my blade to make doors between worlds. This is what I've been training for, and now it's time to use what I've learned.

It's strange how two kingdoms can share my heart so fully, yet it rests completely with one boy.

When we let ourselves be brave, we share our hearts in all kinds of different ways.

Some people steal strange gifts from window displays to mend broken hearts.

Some share home-cooked meals, songs, and stories of their ancestors.

Some help their loved ones through school and ask them to do their homework.

Some prepare their mentees for a thousand dreadful curses, and some even grow pumpkins.

And me . . .? I grab my guitar, find a familiar face in Belhaven on the first day of spring, and I wonder if he recognizes me when we lock eyes.

For a second, he looks as though he's seen a phantom. He walks right past me, does a double-take, and then slowly, he approaches.

I ask if the boy wants to hear a story less

told, about a prince who found *another* prince and how they battled a thousand curses together.

He says he's not quite sure. It depends. Is it like a love story?

I tell him it's only a love story if he wants it to be. Just before midnight on Halloween, he said some magical words, and I finally knew we'd been feeling the same thing. But words aren't quite enough to break a curse.

I think maybe love is action—sharing a friend's burden, shielding another in danger, or letting go of your favorite guitar. At least one of these things saved our lives on Halloween night, because all of them were true love.

But if Isaac has moved on and prefers to hear a ghost story, then I'll learn to let him go, too.

So, my brain turns to goo when Isaac's lips land on mine. The kiss is gentle and lasts no longer than a blink, but stars and gods, it knocks all the wind out of my lungs.

"Do you still want to tell it?" he asks.

And I do, Isaac. I really do.

THE END

ACKNOWLEDGMENTS

A confession: Writing out these thank yous feels harder than writing the book this time, because there was a lot that had to align in my life before I could see all the pieces of the story. In fact, as simple as this one may be, the first ingredients started cooking in my head about ten years ago! *A Thousand Dreadful Curses* is the product of:

- The "spooky-lite" genre of stories that fascinated me as a kid during every Halloween season: R.L. Stine's *Goosebumps* series, movies like *Halloweentown* and *Hocus Pocus*, and others!
- A love for weird fairy tales. This one is loosely inspired by Italo Calvino's telling of *La ragazza mela* or *Apple Girl*, a Florentine folk tale. A queen gives birth to an apple, kicking off a wild ride involving love, jealousy, sorcery, and danger—all in about three pages!
- The writers and creators who are paving

the way for more LGBTQ+ inclusion in middle grade and young adult literature. This has been so encouraging to see!

There are dear friends of mine who are doing great work to build a better world for folx who have ever felt like a "blue pumpkin." They are woven into this book, which isn't enough of a thank you for the work they do! This is also true of my family—I love you all!

I want to thank Silvia Curry for her edits and feedback on this story, as well as Molly Phipps for her work on the cover and interior design! Like Jack and his guitar, you all take words, designs, and ideas and create magic time after time. Thank you!

To my readers: Whether you're discovering me for the first time or you've been reading my books for a while, I appreciate you more than you know!

OTHER BOOKS BY JACOB DEVLIN

The Carver

The Unseen

The Hummingbird

Roses in the Dragon's Den

Brambles in the Wishing Well

ABOUT THE AUTHOR

JACOB DEVLIN is the author of multiple books for teens and pre-teens including *Roses in the Dragon's Den*, which won a Reader's Favorite Silver Medal in 2019. Outside of writing, he enjoys drawing, planning for his next Comic-Con, and spending time with friends and family. He especially looks forward to Halloween every year, when the Arizona weather becomes cool enough to enjoy long walks and warm drinks outside!

Find him online at:
authorjakedevlin.com